D0916151

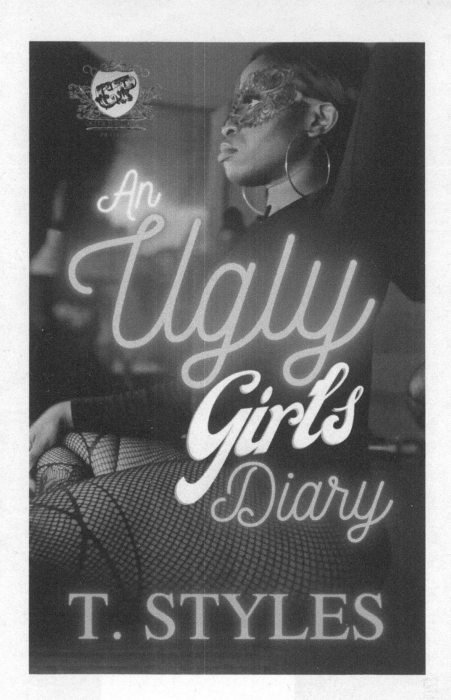

An Ugly Girls Diary

T. STYLES

ARE YOU ON OUR EMAIL LIST?

SIGN UP ON OUR WEBSITE

www.thecartelpublications.com

OR TEXT THE WORD: CARTELBOOKS TO

22828

FOR PRIZES, CONTESTS, ETC.

4

WWW.THECARTELPUBLICATIONS.COM

AN UGLY GIRL'S

DIARY

BY

T. STYLES

PUBLISHER'S NOTE:
This book is a work of fiction. Names,
characters, businesses,
Organizations, places, events and incidents
are the product of the
Author's imagination or are used fictionally.
Any resemblance of
Actual persons, living or dead, events, or
locales are entirely coincidental.

Library of Congress Control Number: 2022914651

ISBN 10: 194837384X

ISBN 13: 978-1948373845

Cover Design: BOOK SLUT CHICK

First Edition

Printed in the United States of America

What Up Famo,

I hope and pray your summer has been going exceptionally well for you so far. Our summer has been non-stop with movie making, but that's a great thing! However, when it was time to jump back into novels, T. Styles is ALWAYS ready.

Which brings me to the book in hand, *An Ugly Girl's Diary*! This new tale gives classic T. Styles energy and had me pulled in from page one! I literally read it in one sitting because I had to find out what was going on. Trust me, make sure you have a few hours available when you sit down with this one 'cuz you're gonna need it!

With that being said, keeping in line with tradition, we want to give respect to a vet, new trailblazer paving the way or pay homage to a favorite. In this novel, we would like to recognize:

MAX JULIEN

Maxwell Julien Banks, better known to us all as *Goldie* from one of my favorite movies, *The Mack*, was an actor, clothing designer and screenwriter. I absolutely LOVED that movie, and no matter what else Max was in after *The Mack* he was always best known for that role. My sister CeCe and I used to watch it and *Uptown Saturday Night*, almost daily when we were younger! We were so saddened by his passing. May he rest in eternal peace! We're grateful that his contribution to cinema will forever live on!

Aight...I'ma let y'all jump in this one here because once you're in it, it won't let you go! Enjoy!

See ya soon!
Charisse "C. Wash" Washington
Vice President
The Cartel Publications
www.thecartelpublications.com
www.facebook.com/publishercwash
Instagram: Publishercwash
www.twitter.com/cartelbooks
www.facebook.com/cartelpublications
www.theelitewritersacademy.com
Follow us on Instagram: Cartelpublications
#CartelPublications
#UrbanFiction
#PrayForCece
#RIPMaxJulien

#ANUGLYGIRLSDIARY

This Is Dedicated To The Unseen

Out of the darkness…
Into the darkness…
To find the light…

CHAPTER ONE
THE SUMMER OF TYE

The weatherman called for a heatwave...

But it didn't impact the people inside of the newly renovated black owned Asian cuisine restaurant in Baltimore named "The Lit".

The invitees were drunk, high, and ready to risk it all.

Inside the dwelling, one of its owners, Tye Gates, sat on the sink within the woman's bathroom. His beautiful fiancé stood a few feet away and was studying and reapplying her makeup in the mirror. Clumps of tissue tinged with red lipstick, blush and blue eyeshadow sat on the sink as she actively removed more.

While he directed the wipe down, music boomed outside of the restroom because a celebration was going on and he couldn't wait to participate. After all, the festivities were going on in his honor.

But first he had to check her ass.

"Is this enough?" Joanne Davenport questioned, wiping her long brown hair out of her face so he could see her glowing cocoa colored skin.

"More..." he said.

"You can be mean...overbearing."

"I said more."

He didn't care that she was trying to reach him through sympathy. You only needed to look at the tattoos on his light brown skin to know what sat in the man's heart. Afterall, there was an italicized tattoo that ripped across his forehead which read DOMINION. The second running along his left cheek read POWER and the third on the right side read RULE.

The artwork, so blatant, connected to one another with brown vines. To be clear it was beautiful to observe and at the same time off-putting in professional settings.

But he didn't give a fuck.

The man was his own boss.

In more ways than one.

Standing over six feet easy, he took care of his body on a daily basis. To say he was chiseled would be lazy. It was better to say that the man was fine and call it a day. Only the best labels touched his skin and only the most expensive oils scented his flesh. He was alluring, which often pulled many women into his self-professed dick trap.

Some old, had fallen to his game.

Others young.

At present he'd been with ninety-nine women.

His current love victim was Joanne, a complex beauty who came with her own share of secrets. After removing what was left of her makeup, she looked over at him. "This...looks..."

"Good."

"No, Tye. It doesn't." She threw her hands up in the air. "You get a kick out of this don't you? Controlling me."

"I told you what I liked in a woman from the gate. You just thought it was a game." His phone vibrated and he removed it from his pocket to read the text.

"Sometimes I feel like you're bored with me."

He looked up from his phone. "Then entertain me more."

"How?"

"If I gotta tell you how to keep my interest, why stay?"

"Because I know something better is in your heart." She grabbed the soiled tissue from the counter as if it were a mound of snow and dumped it in the trash can. Smoothing her hands alongside her gold glitter dress, which hugged at her curves, she observed her reflection in the mirror. "And I'm waiting on you to show me that side."

After sending his text message he hopped off the sink and walked over to her. They observed one another in the mirror. Slowly he took his hand, dipped under her dress, and eased past her pussy lips before finding the soft warm center.

She was wet.

Gliding his finger out, he tasted her juices and whispered into her ear. "Naturally beautiful." He panned her chin to the left and then right. "Naturally fresh. The way I like it."

Her clit jumped. "No such thing. We all have flaws. Even you."

"Nah, I'm perfect." He winked. "Haven't you heard?" He took a deep breath and turned her from the mirror to face him. "When we get out there, I want you to relax a little. And have a good time."

"I always have a–."

"It's a big night for me." He squeezed her shoulders lightly. "Remember that. You're not my wife yet."

"No, but I am your fiancé. It's a big night for me too." Her voice went high and he could tell she was on the verge of ruining his evening by being too emotional already. Something he hated like shit. "Can you be honest and tell me why you're with me? For real."

"You're my fiancé." He tucked a hefty weft of her flowing hair behind her ear and said, "And I want you to be a nigga's wife. But I can't deal with your up and down moods. And your need to put your family in the mix when we go through shit."

She shook her head. "I said I wouldn't do that anymore."

"You said many things. I just want you to remember that niggas don't like that shit. As fine as you are, it's probably the main reason it took you so long to find a real one. Your father be applying too much pressure."

She looked down and back up at him. "Like I said, our relationship is our own. I promise."

He was about to walk away.

"Tye..."

He turned around and faced her.

"Sometimes understanding another's darkness is the best method for knowing yourself."

"Shit sounds stupid."

"It doesn't make it untrue." She paused. "I'll fall to the back. But stay out of trouble, Tye. I don't want to get a call that the police pulled you over and locked you up again."

He chuckled once. "Let's go."

The moment they opened the door, a flood of people greeted them with cheers and well wishes.

The restaurant was so crowded it resembled an upscale night club. There was bubbled paneling on the top part of the walls and silver finishing everywhere. The lights flooded the space with neon pink and blues which could change upon request. Haze pumped everywhere giving the room a romantic fog. Venetian couches ran along the perimeter of the walls and red velvet ropes turned the areas into mini V.I.P. sections. In the center of the floor sat designer tables with Victorian style chairs for dining.

It was spectacular.

As the music boomed, Tye appeared to float in the very center of the dance floor. The flashing strobe lights bounced off his tatted face and his gold chains played in the shine like whores.

There were so many people present that for the moment he felt like a star. Like the hero of his own story and he loved every minute.

While he basked under the lights, his closest comrade and business partner, Logan, bopped up

19

to him with a grin on his face. Without saying a word, he handed him a bottle of ice-cold champagne, with tiny ice shards sliding down the sides. Logan already popped the cork a few seconds before, and so Tye tossed it upward, allowing the suds to run down his throat and the sides of his face.

Winking at Joanne from across the room, she grinned and strutted toward him. "You inviting me into the spotlight already? I thought trophies were better seen and not heard."

His friends gave him room.

Tye wrapped an arm across her lower back and whispered in her ear. "Open."

On cue, she widened her pink pouty lips as he poured the cool liquid down her throat. She'd swallowed his cum on many occasions so she didn't miss a drop. Allowing it to bubble down her throat.

Every man in the room felt envy.

She was beautiful and nasty.

She was a Davenport.

"That was yummy," she said, wiping her mouth with the back of her hand. "I can't wait to eat ice cream later." She ran her hand sneakily across his thickening dick.

20

"Now I'm entertained..." he said looking into her eyes. Turning her around he placed his warm lips against her ear. His words vibrated, causing her drums to tingle. "You see the way every nigga in the building looking at you?"

"Yesssssss." She breathed deeply.

"That's why I chose you. Never forget that shit."

Every eye was on them at the moment.

Turning her back around he kissed her passionately.

Having gotten her orders she said, "I'ma let you enjoy your night," she grinned.

When she switched away, his boys, with Logan in the lead, slapped him on the back in celebration. Rough and rowdy, they were excited to see one of their own finally make it off the streets.

"You did it!" Logan announced to be heard over the music.

"We did it!" Tye corrected him.

"I'm just happy to be on the team!"

Tye poured more champagne down his throat.

"Oh, before I forget, I got something for you!" Logan removed a gift wrapped in black paper with gold specks and handed it to him. Yelling in his ear he said, "This is an original copy of Lilou Dubois' last work before she died."

Tye's eyes widened. "Wait…you…you…"

"Yep!" Logan laughed.

An avid reader, if the book was genuine, which he knew it was since Logan was solid, it would be worth a grand. "How did you…I mean…"

"I know she's your favorite author!" He yelled a bit louder when the beat dropped. "And even though I'm not into the dark shit you read; I know how important it is to you."

Tye handed him the bottle and tore the paper off and allowed it to fall to the floor. The book was beautiful. Bound in leather, the words *'The Lure Of Misery by Lilou Dubois'* were etched on the cover in black. He had been a fan of reading since he was a child so this was a hell of a gift.

Tye wrapped one arm around him, pulled him near and smiled. "Thanks, man! This…this…"

"What's understood doesn't need to be said! I just appreciate you letting me in on this deal at the last minute!"

When Tye looked across the room, he didn't spot his fiancé anymore. But he did spot his mother and sister. His mother wore her usual gold pixie wig and his sister had gold and black box braids running down her back.

Both looked miserable as fuck.

Walking over to them he said, "Y'all good?"

Ava, his sister, looked away.

"Ava...you aight?"

"We here for you." She shrugged. "So...so we good."

He looked at his mother again. "You?"

"We fine, Tye." She raised the cup filled with brown poison toward her lips. "Now go have fun and stop fishing. We gonna be on our best behavior tonight." She looked at her daughter and Ava walked away.

He shook his head. "Listen...I need you to give this to Joanne later." He handed the book to his mother. But only after demanding that she secure it with her life. "Don't lose it."

"I got you, baby," she said proudly. "I know how you are about these books. Now go."

He returned to his friends. As they celebrated his win, his cell phone vibrated. Removing it from his pocket, he looked down at the screen and read the message.

2nite is a big night.
4 both of us.
Remember that when U decide how
quickly to pay what you owe.

Tye tucked the phone back in his pocket and looked around the room. His eyes scanned his restaurant desperately, to see through the darkness for the messenger.

Nothing.

"You good?" Logan asked, a heavy hand on his shoulder. "You look like you expecting to get shot or something."

"Why you say that?" Tye said, being jolted out of his search.

"What you mean?"

"I just wanna know why you said that shit. You trying to ruin my night or something?" Tye's face was serious like Joe Pesci's in the Funny Guy scene from Goodfellas. "I'm waiting, nigga." He remained stone-faced and suddenly burst into laughter.

"Nigga..." Logan chuckled, relieved it wasn't that deep. "I was about to say." He handed the bottle back to Tye. "Get this up in you 'cause you tripping."

"Ain't nobody tripping. I'm having the time of my life!" He gulped half the bottle of champagne.

As he continued to bond with his squad, suddenly he saw a sexy figure that caused his dick

24

to jump, staring at him from across the room. From what he could appraise, she was a gorgeous brown skinned girl wearing a dress so tight she looked like a wrapped candy apple.

Despite the room being packed, she appeared to be staring at him. Like she wanted the dick. Since it was rare to have a stare so intense, he enjoyed the few moments eye-fucking her back.

When one of her friends talked in her ear, she leaned down to catch their words, while maintaining his gaze the entire time. She was a seductress and he enjoyed every minute.

And then something happened.

Candy Apple whispered in a friend's ear, hugged her and the other two women and walked away.

Ah, nah! He thought.

He had planned to eye fuck her from a distance all night. Besides, he couldn't make a move since his girl was somewhere close. So foreplay would have to be it. It was too dangerous to go fishing. And still, the moment she left, he peeled himself away from the crew.

Fuck it. He thought to himself.

He definitely had a type. And in that moment, he was ready to risk it all.

Pushing past all the well-wishers, congrats and touches on the back and shoulder, he found himself outside in the heat which threatened to take his breath away. The weatherman gave Baltimore the warning, but this felt like hell.

Where was she?

From where he stood he looked up and down the block but he didn't spot her thick, curvy frame. He was caught in a thirst trap he couldn't get from up under. Five minutes passed when he realized his dick would not meet a new friend.

Believing he had missed his opportunity to fuck, something he was accustomed to doing even while engaged, he hit it to his silver Benz which sat on the curb to smoke a blunt.

Turning on the air conditioner and radio, he split, stuffed, and ran a lighter along the sides of his blunt to make it stiff. It was completely rolled when he saw the beautiful silhouette of a woman leaning against the wall of an adjacent building.

Black art.

It was Ms. Apple.

Tossing the blunt into the cup holder, he threw his car door open and rushed toward her. The music poured out onto the street as he made his approach. "Leaving so soon?"

26

"Leaving?" She smiled and popped a bubble from the pink gum spinning in her mouth. "How I'm leaving when I'm waiting on my ride?" A brown Neverfull purse with a red interior dangled from the cusp of her arm.

"Does that mean yes?"

She smiled. Her gaze fell on his designer shoes all the way up to his eyes. And then she looked away from him as if no longer entertained.

Playing hard to get right? He thought.

"Come talk to me." He stepped closer. "In my car. I'll take you where you want to go."

She seemed to think about it forever, and his dick jumped in anticipation. "Why you being so nice to me?"

"You wanna ride? Not 'bout to ask you again."

Slowly she walked toward his Benz, and he sped in front of her to quickly open the passenger door. Looking behind him once to be sure Joanne or her nosey ass friends weren't watching, he slipped inside his door which was already open.

She tossed her Neverfull on the floor and positioned herself comfortably in the soft leather seat.

Complete strangers to the night, two minutes later they were cruising down the street like future lovers. Passing some wrecked buildings and many more beautiful ones, he continued quite a way down the Baltimore roads.

Grabbing the blunt he fired it up and inhaled. "Smoke?" He extended it her way.

She didn't resist.

"So what made you come tonight?" He asked.

She inhaled and exhaled. "You mean besides celebrating you opening a black owned Asian restaurant? With like real Chinese food."

Now he was intrigued. "You came for me?"

She handed the blunt back and blew pillows in the air. "A friend of mine dates your friend. And she invited me along." She shrugged. "Plus even though I don't know you directly, I know of you. And you make me proud."

He liked her choice of words.

He continued to sink into his seat. "I'm not gonna lie. I'm taken."

"I said I know you."

"So you know I'm not leaving my girl either then."

She giggled. "What's known doesn't need to be repeated." She reached for the blunt and he handed it to her willingly. "I don't want anything for you I wouldn't want for myself."

"Is that right?"

She pulled and the tip glowed orange. Slowly she released haze into the air. "The question is, Tye, what do you want for yourself?"

He placed a hand on her warm thigh.

Her legs widened as if he had the passcode.

He looked at her and casually pulled into an alley. It was a place he'd gone many times before to conduct "business". So he was quite aware that it was private and more importantly didn't get a lot of traffic. Once he parked, he smashed out the flames of the weed.

"I want to see what you feel like." He spoke, positioning his body to look into her eyes.

She smiled as if she had been wanting to hear his words from the jump. Raising her dress just enough, she removed her panties slowly. Left foot out followed by the right and allowed them to fall on her purse. Next she crawled on top of him and he was already strapped and ready to go.

As her pussy covered his dick, she became number one hundred.

Staring up at her he was impressed with her beauty.

She was flawless.

Absent of tattoos, bruises, or moles.

"The way you look at me is intoxicating," she breathed. "And...I ...I see why."

"You see why what?"

"I see why you inspire so much madness."

He believed she was talking about his girl who came from a unique group of people but he decided not to entertain anything other than the pussy.

After he entered her body, slowly and tucked himself inside right comfortably, he was impressed with the level of tightness. He knew it didn't mean she wasn't having sex but based off of his history he unfortunately ran into more than enough women with loose boxes and foul odors.

This was a treat.

She was a treat.

"You fine as fuck." He spoke the truth. Her body was the evidence.

Hands gripping his seat, she raised up and fell back down slowly. "And so are you."

Gripping her ass cheeks, he slid in and out. He had confidence that no one would bother him in the alley and so he wanted to take his time. Using small repetitions, he continued to move in this way as if warming her up.

"You know how to make it last," she moaned. "I...I like that shit, nigga."

As she delivered him his praises, his lips found her breast which up until that moment had been squeezed by its owner. Now his tongue ran over her nipple and when it hardened, he bit down lightly.

She moaned. "Damn, bro. That feel good as fuck."

Although this was the first time they had been together their chemistry brought with it a rhythm that was erotic. Had they been in a competition they would have been champions.

His thickness remained inside, as her juices poured down his shaft and on to the opening of his boxers like syrup. He loved the way she popped each ass cheek like butterfly wings while going up and down. Next to the book Logan bought him, this was the highlight of the night. A beautiful woman who was grown and didn't need promises of the future to indulge sexually was a gift he didn't deserve.

But it didn't mean he wouldn't take the honor.

He was just about to bust when he noticed her head fall backwards. Normally he would think only of himself and release his load proper like, but she had put in such great craftsmanship that he stopped himself from cumming and gave her the satisfaction of the moment.

Gripping her hips, he waited a few seconds more until he heard her sensuous voice moan loudly. The tone was in the middle of a scream and a cry of pleasure which caused him to release too. Pressing down into one another, they squeezed out each bit of juice until they were staring into one another's eyes.

She had her thoughts.

He had his.

That quickly, now that the moment was over, the realization that he left his party to indulge in a complete stranger rested upon his shoulders. He didn't necessarily suffer guilt but he realized he had to fake it if he were to get back in Joanne's good graces. Especially if she knew he was missing.

Easing off of him, she reclaimed her seat, fixed her clothing, and said, "That was nice."

"Agreed." He reached across her body and grabbed a few tissues. Suddenly she was in the way. Wiping the condom and nut off of his dick he rolled the window down and tossed it outside.

Like most dogs, he was ready to sniff the next thing.

"So...uh...I–."

"Look, I know you're in a rush." She spoke, looking at him from the side. "But I gotta pee right quick. When I get back, hopefully you can take me home."

He winked.

She looked around and said, "I'm gonna pick one of the restaurants and–."

"Just pee in the alley."

She glared. "I'm not an animal."

He nodded, secretly wishing she was. "Do what you gotta." He readjusted the chain on his chest and melted into the seat. "Be swift. I got people waiting on me."

Quickly she exited the car, closed her door, and ran down the street before disappearing out of sight. Tucked in the alley, as each minute passed he was getting anxious. Suddenly he cared about everyone who would be wondering where he went at his restaurant.

Instantaneously he was concerned about his mother, sister, Logan and definitely Joanne.

Ten minutes passed...

He looked around, and she still hadn't returned.

Fifteen minutes...still nothing.

This woman had him fucked up if she thought he would be waiting forever.

Twenty minutes...

"Slim, I don't know you like that for real." He decided he would pull off. "Good luck getting home."

Throwing the car in drive, he was annoyed when he looked down and saw her purse was still in his ride. Why hadn't she bothered to take it with her? Instead of leaving it with a stranger.

No worries...

Easing out of the car, he ran to the passenger's side door. Pulling it open, he grabbed her purse and tossed it into the dark alley behind a trash can. If you didn't have business there, which most people didn't, he reasoned it would be safe. And he hoped Candy Apple was up for a little scavenger hunt when she returned.

Because he was bouncing.

After making sure the designer purse was not visible to the naked eye, he pulled off.

That was the least he could do.

Now it was time to perform.

Hitting the phone on his car, he called his fiancé's work number, which he had done before.

Of course he knew she wasn't there. She was at the party, possibly waiting on him.

He was famous for calling her work to fake "reach" her. And whenever she asked why he did that, when he knew she wasn't at work, he claimed he had both numbers programmed under her name. And that it was a mistake. When in actuality it was a way to leave a message without hearing her mouth.

Before performing, he took a deep breath.

Now he was ready. "Bae! Bae! I was dropping one of my friends off and the cops pulled me over. FUCK! Why can't they leave us the fuck alone! A black man ain't safe out here! I'll let you know if they arrest me. I'm sorry."

He knew like most of the world that there was no greater conflict than a black man and a police officer. And in that moment he used it to his advantage, before pulling off with a smile on his face.

CHAPTER TWO
GOLD BOUND

Tye was fast asleep on his couch when he felt cold water spray on his face.

Jumping up, he saw his fiancé standing before him with a spray bottle. Even though she was angry, she looked beautiful with her hair swept up in a ponytail which ran down her back. Not to mention she was wearing the red negligée he loved.

Frowning, she sprayed him again. "Where were you, Tye?"

"Stop spraying me! And why did you do that shit!"

"I asked you a question." She sprayed him once more and he snatched it from her and tossed it on the sofa.

Grabbing her wrist he said, "Calm down!"

She pulled away. "You left your party and went only God knows where and then when you came home you didn't come to our bed. What is wrong with you?"

He stood up and walked toward the luxury kitchen. Their apartment was huge with three bedrooms, two bathrooms and a kitchen with an island running down the center. And at that moment he wished she was in any other room instead of being up in his face.

He hit the button to the coffee maker hoping it would hurry to give him the pickup he needed. "Did you check your voice message?"

"What?"

"I said did you check your shit? Because I called you and left a message."

"Tye...where were you that you had to message me?"

"Went to drop off a friend and got pulled over by the police."

Her eyes lowered. "I didn't get any message."

"Then that's on you." He grabbed a cup and sat it on the counter. "But I did call."

She placed her hands on her hips. "Why did you leave? To even be pulled over by the police in the first place."

"He came to celebrate, and his baby mother went into labor."

"What friend?"

His eyes widened because he hadn't thought about this part. It couldn't be a friend she knew because she would verify. It was time to make one up. Glancing at a book on the table he read the author's name and said, "Matthew. So it's not my–."

"Why do bad things always happen to you?"

He glared. "Are you calling me a liar?"

"You are known for lying."

He glared harder. "Careful."

She took a deep breath. "Let me guess, you called my work number again?" She chuckled once. "This shit is starting to sound fake."

"You not my wife yet. I don't have to answer to you." He said, now facing her.

"Okay, listen, I get you're in one of the biggest time frames in your life. But you will not disrespect me the way that you did last night again. Ever. Because whether I love you or not I will leave you."

He extended his hand and pulled her toward him. Since he was only wearing plaid pajama pants and no shirt, her warm body pressed against his muscles. "I will never do that again. I promise."

"What won't you do again, Tye? I need you to be specific."

"I won't step out if we're together without letting you know first."

She took a deep breath. It was good enough for her. It always was.

She increased her height by standing on her tiptoes and kissed his lips. "Oh, before I forget, I have your book. Logan said your mother gave it back to him. I put it on the bookshelf."

"That's right." Tye walked into the living room and toward his shelf. It was massive and took up one side of the living room, running from right to left.

On the shelf were books from when he was a child to the present and it included classics from *Edgar Allan Poe* all the way to urban fiction superstars like *K'wan, Wahida Clark* and more. But it was the recent book that Logan bought him that he loved the most. Holding the copy in his hand, he flipped it open and ran his fingers over the print.

He developed a love for reading after growing up in a dark environment as a child. The stories took him away and allowed him to dream of something better. Something different.

"Breakfast," Joanne yelled from the background.

"What?" His eyes continued to cover the texture of the paper.

"I want you to buy me breakfast," she walked alongside him. "You owe me that since your ass stayed out all night."

"I thought you were cooking."

"Nah...you fucked that up. New plan. Breakfast from Auntie Reese's."

Fifteen minutes later, Tye was sitting in his car holding his book. He had placed an order and was waiting for it to be prepared. He was just about to dig in when he saw a tiny tear off the condom he used under his foot.

Many men had gotten caught cheating from the little corner of a condom wrapper. Quickly he picked it up and tossed it out the window. Next he exited his car to do a quick scan of the driver's area. When he was sure the coast was clear and clean, he did the same on the passenger's seat. Opening the door, he was stunned when he saw a gold leather bound book which was kept together by an elastic band.

Picking it up, he held it between his fingertips. "Fuck is this?"

Examining the book, he closed the passenger's door and eased into his seat to evaluate it fully. His favorite French author would have to wait.

Releasing the band of the book, he opened the cover. The first six words breathed him in...

****

January 15, 2008, 7:00 PM
This is an ugly girl's diary...

He closed the book and looked around.

He didn't even realize why he was suddenly so cautious. It wasn't like he'd stolen the book. Sure he fucked who he believed to be its owner and tossed her purse on the ground. But still, that, in his opinion, was his only crime.

Opening the diary again, he continued to read...

****

January 15, 2008, 7:00 PM

This is an ugly girl's diary. Don't bother telling me it ain't true cause I won't believe

41

you. My eyes are too far apart. My weight ain't been steady since my mama died and the only thing cute on me is the strawberry patch tattoo on my left shoulder. I got it after...

Tye slammed the diary closed.

The woman he fucked the night before didn't have a tattoo. She was beautiful. She didn't have a single flaw. So how could the book belong to her?

Could it be that she found it just like he did?

Maybe even stolen it?

He reopened the diary...

I got it after my aunt had her 60th birthday party. Out of all the gifts she got, and she got a bunch, she liked my strawberry birthday cake the best.

She's my only friend.

How pathetic.

Right?

Maybe that's why so many bad things keep happening to me.

But I do have a favorite cousin. Her name is Penny. And she loved me so much I felt like my heart couldn't handle the attention.

She did things that only people who love you do.

She told me I was pretty when she combed my hair. She would always give me the second half of her steak and cheese from Tasha's Carryout, even though I knew she loved her food. And she would always fight for me if anybody talked bad about me while she was around.

So why did I let Nicole, my other cousin, convince me to play The Crying Game with her boyfriend last night? Which won't do anything but ruin our bond.

I don't know.

I hate myself sometimes when I remember it all.

No, scratch that, I hate myself every day.

I'm thinking maybe if I write down what happened, how it happened, the shit won't hurt so bad.

Here goes.

I was in my room listening to music when Cousin Nicole knocked on the door. Up until that point I always thought she liked me too.

But Diary, you should know that I am a bad judge of character in advance.

The worst things and worse people always seem to find me. I could be hiding in my room, and something that means to do me harm will sniff me out.

That's what happened the other day.

When she knocked, I slipped off my headphones and I opened the door. She was wearing the t-shirt we bought at Hot Topic last week. It was white with a huge yellow smiley face on the front. I remember thinking that her long black hair made the smiley face look as if it had hair too.

Just on the sides though.

"What you doing?" She asked.

I should have known something was up then. She never asked me what I was doing. She'd just push inside and flop on my bed like I wasn't paying part of the rent with her and Penny.

"Nothing...why?"

"You love Penny, don't you?"

"I do."

"How much?"

"I don't know what you mean."

She rolled her eyes. "Well she's about to marry Greg."

I didn't know. "Is that bad? Greg is always nice to me and–."

"That's 'cause you don't know everything. Penny don't talk to you like she does me. You don't even come out your room half the time."

It was true.

"If she marries him it will be bad. Really bad. And then she'll leave our apartment. I don't know about you but I can't afford the rent in a halfway split with you."

She knew I didn't want Penny to leave. But I still wanted her to be happy because nice people deserved it so much. She didn't say much yet. But my head was thumping like I was about to set myself up.

I just didn't know how.

"So what can we do?"

Now she pushed her way inside and closed my door. Leaning against it she said, "The Crying Game."

My eyes widened with fear.

That's the danger I knew was coming.

I've seen The Crying Game played before. Nicole was famous for pulling it out for every reason under the sun. The last time she did it was aimed against her best friend Dana. And if

I remember correctly, they hadn't spoken since. If it wasn't for her best friend Lala, she wouldn't have no friends.

Just...like...me.

"You going to do The Crying Game on Greg?"

"No." A long finger pointed my way. "You are."

"Me? But...but I'm no good with people."

"That's not true. You're plenty good. You just don't know it."

I was afraid.

After all, standing next to my cousin Nicole and Penny, I was the last person a man would look at. And the rules of The Crying Game were simple. First you had to be able to seduce.

And I couldn't seduce anyone to do shit.

The way it worked was like this...when it is believed that a boyfriend is being unfaithful or a cheater, one of the participants has to come on to him to prove if it's true. If he accepts the offer, which usually is sex, the participant is supposed to let the girlfriend know before things get out of hand.

If the girlfriend is strong enough she's supposed to end the relationship.

46

But I knew what it felt like to be lonely. And even if my boyfriend cheated, which as you know I don't got one anyway, I wouldn't care.

So I would take him back.

Every time.

That's just me.

Like I was saying, in order for the game to be effective the man had to be attracted to the participant. And there was nothing I knew that said that Greg was attracted to me.

"I don't wanna do it."

"But didn't you just hear what I said?" Spit flew across the room as she yelled. "It will help Penny. I mean, who wanna marry a nigga who will eventually break her heart anyway?"

"Why can't you do it?"

"Because I seen him looking at you. He likes you a lot."

There was my excuse gone out the window.

I wanted to run.

But I couldn't. Like a bird in a cage I was trapped. And there was no way out of this. Even if I left to visit my aunt or I went to dance in my private place, she would be here waiting on me.

I knew that more than anything.

Nicole always got what she wanted.

But that night Nicole wanted my soul.

"I won't have sex with him."

"Girl, ain't nobody want you to fuck him. That ain't how The Crying Game works anyway. Right before he puts it in, knock on the door so I can walk in and catch him red handed."

"But what about Penny?"

"She at work. She ain't coming home early."

And so I let her convince me to do what I felt was wrong. I wore my tight ripped up jeans and the shirt Nicole was wearing. I preferred to wear my own clothes, but she said he liked girls to be innocent and so the smiley face shirt would do the trick. I remember smelling the places where her sweat dampened the underarm parts when she had it on.

It made me want to throw up.

Moist and uncomfortable, I kept it on anyway.

Within a few moments of me getting dressed there was a knock at the door. It was firmer, harder, and up higher so I knew it was him.

"You in there?" He yelled.

"Uh...yes." I opened it up after taking a bit too long. How did she even convince him to knock on my door in the first place?

"Where the picture you want hung?" He was 6'6, dark skinned and muscular.

That's how.

Me and Penny had a lot in common. We both had light brown skin. But I'm 5'7 and she's 5'5 and I always wondered how they worked it in the bedroom because he was so much bigger than her.

He clapped once. "Where the picture?"

I grabbed him by his hand and brought him inside, before closing the door behind him. I was a bit too rough because if I hurried, at least this whole thing would be over quick.

"What you doing?" He pulled his hand out of mine. "And didn't Nicole have on that shirt earlier?"

That was embarrassing.

"I just wanted to talk to you."

"About what?" He seemed irritated. I don't blame him. What I also noticed was that it didn't feel like he wanted me like Nicole said.

I know now she lied.

I didn't know what else to do so I raised up on my tiptoes and kissed him on the chin. Then I knocked on the door twice. That was code for Nicole to come in and catch him.

She didn't come though.

She didn't save me.

I wish she had.

At first, during our kiss, his massive palms pressed against my chest. But then something I'll never forget happened. He took his hand and pushed it on the top of my head.

Roughly.

My lips brushed down his chin, the cloth of his chest and I slammed down on my knees.

I can't say I was a willing participant at this point.

"Oh, so this what you wanna do huh?" He said harshly, looking at the door once before staring down at me. "You wanna taste a nigga's dick, baby girl? I'ma let you do it too."

With one hand behind my head, and the free one on himself, he unzipped his pants and forced his way into my mouth. He was large. Big. Hairy. My teeth hurt and my heart broke as he pushed in and out. I was devastated. Not because of the pain I was in, I felt that was

50

punishment for my betrayal. To be honest I'm used to things like this happening to me.

I felt bad for Penny. She deserved a boyfriend better than him.

I even allowed myself to say, maybe Nicole was right. Maybe we did need to get him away from her.

It wasn't even two minutes before I felt a warm salty liquid roll down my throat and make its way to my gut. When it was all said and done he shoved me off and zipped up his pants.

"Get off me, freak!" He pointed my way as his dick softened like ice cream melting in the sun. "You better hope I don't tell Penny this shit. You ain't nothing but a whore."

He didn't have to tell Penny. Because when he opened the door she was there standing next to Nicole. While I was on the floor soiled with his cum which managed to drip on my chin and Nicole's stinky t-shirt.

"What's going on in here?" Penny had tears in her eyes.

She knew exactly what happened.

I tried to think on my feet and tell her what happened. About The Crying Game. About Nicole coming to me about catching Greg doing

51

wrong so she wouldn't marry him. About how she deserved better. But her attention was directed off me as she hit Greg several times with tight fists and wild arms.

He tried to plead with her. Told her it was all my fault and he couldn't resist. At that moment it appeared that she wasn't listening to him.

She ushered him toward the door with screams and small knotted fists, as I remained on the floor, like trash waiting to be taken to the dumpster.

It felt like forever but Penny came back to me.

"Why, cousin?" She cried. "I loved you."

"I thought you were at work." It was a stupid response. Later I'd learn that she was coming home early and Nicole knew.

It was all a set up.

But why?

At that moment though, I spent hours trying to tell her what happened. I saw periods of her believing me, while I made her dinner, followed by more periods of silence before she later threw up.

In the end she shook her head and left me where I was.

Alone in my own betrayal.

In a stinky smiley face shirt.

With a piece of his hair on my tongue.

Tye closed the diary...

He couldn't believe how he was pulled into such a suspenseful and vivid account of someone else's life. But what hit him the most was the time on the dashboard of his car.

He had spent two hours reading a stranger's diary. Entry after entry. If Joanne didn't think he was cheating before she would definitely believe it now. And so, it was time for him to come up with a new plan.

First he ordered lunch instead of the breakfast he abandoned. Then he bought flowers and a bottle of her favorite wine. Sauvignon Blanc. When he was done he dipped home to make things right.

With food and bags in his hands, he rushed up the stairs leading to his apartment. But when he got inside, he saw her singing happily.

What the fuck?

He was preparing to tell her a big lie, something he'd done many times before until she said, "Hey you. What you doing here?" She was in a good mood.

Why?

"I came to bring you food. I ran into one of my suppliers at the restaurant and made a stop."

"Tye, that's so sweet. But I thought you'd still be over your mother's house. I know how they are when they get to fighting and shit."

It wasn't until that time that he realized he didn't bother to look at his phone. Had he looked at his cell he would have definitely gone there first. His mother and sister stayed fighting one another which caused him to play referee. If he didn't provide blockage they would kill each other. On many occasions their fights resulted in hospital visits. And so Joanne assumed this was the reason he didn't come directly back with breakfast.

"Oh yeah, I got that message." He lied. "I just wanted to stop here right quick to get you something to eat. I'm going back now."

She kissed him on his lips and smiled wider. "Well, thank you for thinking of me first. Hopefully things aren't as bad as your mother made them out to be on the phone."

Tye hoped so too but he was definitely prepared for the worst.

CHAPTER THREE
DOMINION, POWER, RULE

The moment Tye walked up the stairwell inside the small Baltimore apartment building, he could hear his mother and sister screaming at the top of their lungs. Before continuing to ascend up the stairs, he leaned against the wall and dragged his hand down his face.

"Swear I don't feel like dealing with this shit."

Since he could remember his mother and younger sister never got along. It was worse when his father, Oliver, was in the picture. A member of an infamous biker gang, The Dominion, he had beaten and abused Tye's mother, Margie, since they first met in high school.

Margie always thought when they had children things would change, It didn't. Instead, he would use different vices to gaslight her into believing that she was the reason their marriage didn't work.

Eventually he did whatever he wanted.

But kept her around.

Oliver's need to control her was the reason she befriended alcohol which fell quickly into a habit which consumed her soul. When her looks disappeared due to a daily intake of liquor, Oliver left his family and bedded his female counterparts in the motorcycle club instead.

He had been absent ever since.

Unless he was bored and wanted an adventure.

After getting himself together, finally Tye trudged up the remaining stairs and used the key to enter their apartment. The moment he crossed the threshold, an iron came flying across his face. Had he come in a moment later he would've been burned and struck for playing hero.

"Fuck is wrong with you!" He yelled at Ava who tried to hit her mother with the object. He closed the door and locked it behind himself.

"She's what's fucking wrong with me!" Her long gold braids ran down her brown skin. "And I hate her! I fucking hate her!"

Ava may have been short in stature, but she was as violent as any rabid dog. And she had tried to kill her mother many a day.

"You see that bitch!" Margie yelled, cowering in the corner. "You see what she just did? Throw a hot iron at her own mother! What kind of disrespectful shit is that? Huh? You tell me that!"

"Ma, just stop." He yelled walking over to her. "She's your daughter."

"She ain't my mother! Trying to steal my money so she can toss liquor down her wrinkled ass throat." She snatched her purse off the counter and shoes off the floor.

"You ain't supposed to be having no money no how! You only sixteen! Might as well give it to me."

"Fuck you! You hear me? Fuck you!" She ran toward the door.

"Where you going?" Tye yelled.

"Aw let her go! All she gonna do is sit on the front porch and beg somebody to drag her whore ass away. I hope they do it too! 'Cept this time don't bring her back!"

Ava screamed and rushed out.

Margie got off the floor and flopped on the sofa. Tye sat next to her. "Y'all gotta stop doing all this dumb shit, ma. It's goofy."

"I know, son, I know."

He placed his hands over hers, which were clenched in her lap. She was trembling and he figured she didn't have her liquor for the day. "I just...I don't know how to get through to her. She doesn't...she doesn't..." her head dipped.

"What, ma?" He squeezed her hand with one of his palms.

"Respect me."

58

He nodded.

Placing a hand on the side of his face she said, "You look so much like your father."

Tye hated that shit. "I hear that a lot. But only from you."

"It's true. You even...you even adopted his club's motto." She rubbed her finger along the tats on his face. "Dominion, power, and rule. Are you cruel to women too?"

He shrugged and took a deep breath. "That's when I didn't know any better."

"You know better now?"

He looked down. "Do you? I mean, are you still letting him use your credit?"

She was embarrassed. "He has his house on my credit but it's destroyed now anyway. So who cares what he puts in my name."

"Ma, you–."

"Tye, please let it go. When you love a person as long as I have, it ain't as easy as you think."

"You gotta stop all this. You gotta stop putting all that clown makeup on your face and put down the glass. And you gotta leave pops alone. You'll find somebody who–"

"I want your father. Is there something wrong with that?"

He shook his head. It was no use. "Any idea where Ava going?"

"Some nigga she fucking. The one I know is twenty something years old and she thinks I don't know." She shook her head. "Just shameful."

He didn't feel she had any room to talk.

"Had the nerve to follow her in the bathroom one day. Pussy stank so bad it smelled like a fisherman's wharf."

He glared. "Ma, I ain't trying to hear all that. Just give me the address."

She grinned. "When you get her, beat her ass for me too. She almost killed your mama. Funky bitch!"

Tye sat outside of Ava's boyfriend's apartment building. His mother only had the location but not the unit. Since he needed more details, he decided to sit in front of the entrance and make a call.

Dialing from his car he said, "You got fifteen minutes to come out of this building, or I'm coming in, Ava. Knocking on every door until I find you too. Don't fuck with me. I ain't ma."

He was sick of his mother and sister with the beefing shit. Forcing him to get involved. But at the moment there was nothing else he could do.

After calling his sister he hit Joanne. "I'll be home when I get my sister out of this nigga's house."

She sighed. "I'm sooooo sorry, Tye. They both gotta grow the fuck up. Seems like it's been getting worse over the years."

"You telling me."

"What is wrong with your family?"

He frowned. "My family? What about yours?"

"Sorry, I just–."

"I'll see you later."

"That's the plan." She sighed.

After ending the call with her he looked over to the right. In the passenger seat of the car sat the diary. It appeared to call him and so, with time to spare, he opened the cover.

****

January 22, 2008, 5:13 PM

Dear Diary,

61

Nicole said I would pay.

Pay for how I treated Penny. She seemed comfortable with leaving out how she tricked me. Tricked me into being with Greg. Tricked me into thinking it was for Penny's own good.

What's worse is that I don't know why she is this way.

How can people who are so mean to one another exist?

I don't understand it all.

Unlike Nicole who terrorized me every day, I hadn't heard anything from Penny. She went to work at night and in the morning she avoided me altogether. I tried to catch her, to give her my side of the story again but she was always quicker.

But Nicole never forgot about me.

It was like she was trying to make me forget her part in it all.

One night she cornered me in the kitchen and showed me how much she wanted to hurt me.

"You know Penny hates you right?" She was smiling high.

"I know."

62

"You should have knocked on the door when he stuck his dick in your mouth. I would've stopped it from going so far. But I guess you wanted to fuck him."

"I did knock!"

"Was it loud?"

"Yes! Why didn't you tell Penny the truth? That it was The Crying Game? So she could stop being mad at me."

"Do you want to know the truth?"

"Of course I do!"

"I didn't tell her because to be honest when the door opened, it looked like you had fun. Like you enjoyed yourself with her boyfriend. To the point where I started to wonder if I could trust you myself."

Hearing her answer caused my stomach to turn. "Of course you can trust me! I only did it to prove my trust."

She crossed her arms over her chest. "I'm going to need more."

"I can't do The Crying Game again."

"We off of that now. Your fuck game was probably trash anyway."

My stomach growled. "Okay so what do you want?"

She moved closer to the refrigerator and pulled it open. "Did I ever tell you about my college days?"

She told me all the time. But I knew she was going somewhere so it was best not to add details that she would give me anyway. "No."

"Me and my soror's were very close."

That was a lie. I hardly ever saw anyone around here. Not even her friends accept Lala.

"But it wasn't that way in the beginning. We had to prove ourselves to each other first." She turned and opened the drawer and grabbed a large spoon. Then she moved to the refrigerator and pulled out mayonnaise. Slowly she took off the top and then picked up ketchup and a can of open sardines that I'm not sure how long had been inside.

My eyes widened. "Then what was enough?"

She mixed the concoction. When she was done, she placed them on the hard marble kitchen counter. "Looks yucky, but I had to do things I didn't want to do. And if you want me to believe you, that you didn't want to fuck Greg, you have to do nasty things too." She slid the jar to me. "It'll make us closer. Like sisters."

64

I was now holding the jar in my hand but not believing my ears. Was she actually asking me to do something so disgusting?

"Before you say you don't want to, understand if you don't then I will tell Penny what else I saw. And I'm sure you don't want that since you love her so much. Oh, and don't throw up in here either!"

"What are you asking?"

"Eat. Every drop."

I was trembling.

At first I didn't understand what the sensation was. But it wouldn't be the last time I felt it. It was rage. Not feeling sorry for myself. Not feeling sorry for someone else.

Just rage.

I fisted the spoon. It wasn't until that time that I realized she picked the biggest spoon in the drawer.

The first bite was disgusting. The second bite was worse. By the third I felt my stomach about to give up on the task.

"Don't throw up in here!" Nicole warned again seeing my expression. Cheeks bubbled. Eyes squinted.

I don't know how I finished the entire jar. I guess I thought about what I had done to Penny. And how much I loved her. And how guilty I felt. But I did finish the whole thing and left the apartment.

As I ran down the hallway, I could hear her laughing the entire way. Like she was at a comedy show and was really enjoying herself. Why did she take such pleasure in things like this? What happened to her to make her this way? And what happened to me to make me be the willing victim?

Of course I knew the answer.

I was always and forever lonely.

Standing on the side of our brick building, I was throwing up so much that I suddenly felt something else was wrong. At first I thought the redness in the goop coming out of me was ketchup. But soon I tasted something else.

Blood.

This felt like the worst day of my life.

And then something happened to make it the best day instead.

I saw someone park any kind of way on the street. He pushed the driver's door open and rushed toward me. "Are you aight?"

66

As I released my gut, I saw he was perfect. And even as he looked at me with eyes red from smoking something that sat in his clothes and gave off a strange funk, I felt there was so much more to him.

I wiped my mouth with the back of my hand. "I don't feel well. But I'll be okay."

He moved closer. He was taller than me but not the tallest guy in the world. And for some reason I imagined myself being pulled into a hug. So tight I breathed in everything on his jacket, leaving it clean.

Probably nasty too since I had vomit everywhere.

"How old are you?"

"Nineteen. How old are you?"

He smiled. "Twenty. Want me to help you back in the house?"

"I can't go back inside."

"Well I was on my way to—"

"I don't expect you to help me. I said I'll be fine."

"How you sound? You're coming with me."

"I don't even know you."

"The name is Peter." He smiled. "You coming now?"

Before I realized it I was at the hospital and confused. I mean what was I going to tell them? That I ate a jar of nasty mayonnaise mixed with other disgusting things due to guilt?

I told them just that.

I told him that too.

I left out the part where I sucked Greg's hairy dick.

When I relieved myself of my burden, I could be wrong, but I felt like there was zero judgment in his eyes.

Did I say that he was high?

Did I say that I wanted whatever he was smoking?

What shocked me the most was not that he took me to the hospital. Any good Samaritan would have done the same right? What shocked me was that he stayed and waited on me. And when I told him again that I didn't want to go home we ended up at the Baltimore National Harbor instead.

I lived here all my life and I have never seen such beauty. And definitely not at night. The colorful skyline sparkled against the water leaving spreading neon globes everywhere.

We talked for what seemed like forever. And it made me feel good.

As my stomach still bubbled, I realized I wanted this feeling to last.

Spoiler alert.

It didn't.

No spoiler alert...it never does.

Tye closed the diary.

He was still sitting outside the building he believed his sister was in with a grown ass man.

Although he didn't know the stranger in the diary, there was something about her that pulled him into her plight. He was so eager to get back to the pages that he quickly went inside the building just as his sister was coming out.

He grabbed her by the arm. "You coming with me."

"No I'm not neither!"

"Don't make me fuck you up out here!" He pointed in her face. "Now let's go."

He got her in his car, kicking and screaming.

She even said some hateful shit he couldn't forget.

But instead of being angry with her like he would have done in the past, he left her to her own madness.

For the moment anyway.

CHAPTER FOUR
FEW DAYS LATER
RUN

Tye drove down the street with a huge order of Peking duck and rice from Joanne's favorite restaurant. She was on the speakerphone as he maneuvered down the dark road. He was wearing a grey sweatsuit with the words "The Lit" on the back in orange which he and Logan got when they launched their restaurant.

"...and I know what you think, Tye. And I'm not saying that you're wrong."

"You don't know what I'm thinking."

"You're thinking that we're spending too much money."

He took a heavy breath and sank deeper into his leather seat. The red stoplight shined on him, casting a glow on his tatted face. There were things he hadn't shared with Joanne. For starters, to get her on his arm he presented in life as someone who had access to a lot of money.

And if he wanted Joanne Davenport, he had to have money.

She came from a long line of people who lived luxuriously. While he, on the other hand, came from the streets. So he fed her the story of a man who was trying to make shit right. And so he borrowed from here and there, moved a few keys and then met someone who would eventually give him the paper he needed to get his business.

But he was still, for the most part, broke.

"I never said it was about the money." He went through the green light.

"I know you didn't say it. It's just that...well...you're asking a lot about the budget and all I want is for our wedding to be beautiful. I want our wedding day to be–."

"Stop making excuses. You want what you want." He looked at the bags of food in his passenger seat when he hit a bump in the road. When he dealt with women before Joanne they would be happy with a few meals and nights out on the town. But she wanted to sustain the lifestyle she was accustomed. And he was starting to get annoyed.

Suddenly he began to laugh.

"What's funny?"

"Nothing, I'm just thinking about something. I mean, lately you been eating out so much it makes me wonder how you gonna even fit in that wedding dress."

Silence.

"Joanne."

"I'm here."

"You heard what I–."

"I heard you, Tye. And I am careful about my looks. I know how important they are to you even though I don't understand why."

He sighed. "It's okay for you to bring up the wedding but not me, huh?" He made a left into their luxury apartment complex.

"I mean, I asked you to get some food from the restaurant because I don't have time to cook with me planning the wedding and–."

"I get all that. But..."

Tye stopped talking when he pulled up in the driveway of his residence, only to see a face he didn't want to see.

"Tye. Are you there?"

"Uh, yeah. I'll be up with your food in a sec."

"So we talking and all of a sudden you ain't got time for me no more?"

"Joanne, I'll–."

"Keep the duck, bitch!"

He ended the call and eased out of his Benz to approach Run Mitchell, the man who loaned him the money. His light skin was more tatted up than his and he was one thousand percent more vicious.

"There's my friend." Run said, with a smile on his face. "What have you been up to?" He extended his hand but it remained outward and unshaken.

"What you doing here, Run? I said I'd get up with you when the time was right. Guess what, it ain't right."

He lowered his hand. "Is that any way to talk to a business partner?"

"Business partner? You kicked me some cash but we ain't partners."

Run laughed once. "You're right. Tomato...toma-toe. But let me remind you how this all started. I was at a bar and you–."

"I know how it started!"

"It's obvious you don't, NIGGA!" He yelled, with spit flying out of his mouth. "I was at a bar and watched you gamble more than you could pay. And they were about to break every bone in your body." His eyes widened with rage. "And I stepped in that night and settled your bet. That means I saved your fucking life. You should be on your knees sucking my dick."

"Nigga, what?"

Run pulled his weapon but kept it hung low. Like a third ball. "You owe."

Tye took a deep breath. He wasn't Superman so if them bullets flew he would be in trouble. "I find it real convenient that when I made my bet that you picked up the pieces. Now you asking—."

"Nah, you asked me for more time to settle the first loan. I granted you that. Next thing I know, you asked for another loan to open your spot."

He shook his head. "I get all that. But the bet was fifty G's. And now somehow I owe a hundred thousand?"

"Interest."

"I wish I never met you."

"But you did though." He pointed a stiff finger into his chest and a heavy hand on his shoulder. "You did. And as a result you were able to open a restaurant that from what I'm hearing has lines around the corner every night. That means you got the girl and the paper. But what that leave me?"

"I need a little more time."

"Convince me to give it to you."

"You already getting interest."

"Getting what I'm due and getting something new are two totally different things. Not only have you made a success of yourself with my money but now I hear you're breaking the bank for some wedding."

His eyes widened. "So that's what this is about? The wedding has nothing to do with what I owe you and–"

"Yes the fuck it does!" He yelled, causing his skin to redden like the flesh of an apple. "Your life is going on without a problem while I'm sitting here waiting like Johnny Gill."

"Run, all I'm saying is that I don't understand why the date changed. We had an agreement."

"It changed when you decided to bump up the grand opening. The agreement was always the opening. You told me that you wouldn't be opening until four months down the line. And then I learn, not from you, that that changed."

"So you got some flunky watching me?"

"You're always being watched, Tye. You're a star. A legend." He paused. "And regardless of how I do my business, it's still my business."

Tye was done. "So what the fuck you want right now? Me to give you the wedding stash? Is that what you saying?"

"Is it enough cash?"

It wasn't.

"Nah."

"Then why the fuck would I want that shit?"

Tye sighed. "I'll pay you in–."

"You have until next Friday to give me the money. Then you'll owe fifty more, bringing the total to one hundred fifty thousand. Or I'll start doing things that will bring heat down on you. Maybe fuck your bitch. Maybe fuck your business partner." He laughed. "I may even fuck you."

Tye saw black. "I respect your position, but I need you not to threaten me like that again. Because if it's gonna be all that, you can just pull the trigger."

"Says the man who never felt a hot slug ever." He laughed. "Give me my money." He tucked his gun in the back of his pants, walked to Tye's car, reached inside, and took the food. "Or else."

He got into his car and drove away.

"How did he know I had food?" Tye mouthed to himself.

CHAPTER FIVE
CHEEKS

After being approached by Run outside, Tye went back to the restaurant to get his fiancé's food. But he also stopped by a bar on his way home since Run blew his entire night and he wanted a drink.

Walking into his house with the second order of Peking duck, the moment he crossed the threshold he could feel Joanne's anger even though she was nowhere in sight.

Slowly he moved toward the bedroom door and twisted the knob. Shaking his head he sighed deeply.

The door was locked.

"Bae...open the door. I know you not in there still mad."

Silence.

He twisted the knob as if the lockout had been a mistake. "Open the fucking door!"

"No!" She yelled from the other side. "Because I'm sick of you saying you'll do one thing and doing another. I'm sick of you lying to me when–."

78

"I got your fucking food!" He raised the bag and dropped it on the floor as if she could see it. "So open the–."

"Go away, Tye!" She cried harder. "Please, just...just go!"

"You know, this is why I don't fuck with you." He pointed several times into the door. "This is why I wasn't sure if...if–"

"If what?" She sniffled.

"If shit don't work out with us and this wedding, now you'll know why."

"So you're threatening not to marry me now?"

"If you want my answer, open this door, mule face bitch!"

"Mule face?!"

"Open the door!"

"You can be so fucking mean! And every time you're like this I tell myself that there has to be a reason. That there has to be a cause for you to be so cruel. I mean, is it your mother or your father and–."

"DON'T BRING MY FUCKING PARENTS INTO THIS SHIT!" He roared. "What's going on now is because you in there acting like a bitch!"

"Just because my feelings are hurt don't mean I'm a bitch. Or weak."

"You don't have any reason to have your feelings hurt. There are people out here going through real shit and you're fucking spoiled." He pointed at the door again. "You hear me? Spoiled!"

"What are you talking about?"

"When I stop coming home, understand it's all on you." Angry, he knocked hard, picked the bag up off the floor and stormed away.

Walking into the kitchen, he removed the food from the bags and warmed it up. Placing it on expensive dishes, he sat it on the table, removed his shirt and rushed outside to his car to grab the diary.

Walking back upstairs, he sat on the sofa, grabbed his plate, and opened the cover.

****

February 15, 2008, 9:27 PM
Dear Diary,

The music was loud and everyone sounded like they were having a good time without me. Nobody bothered to ask if I wanted to come to the party they were having in our apartment.

But why would they?

I was known as the girl who tried to fuck her cousin's man.

They made me an outcast.

Which is a place I felt comfortable these days.

When my landline rang I almost thought it was a mistake. Outside of my aunt I rarely got phone calls. Looking at my pink handset sideways I was so sure it was an error that when the call stopped I proved myself right.

It was a wrong number, I thought.

But it rang again.

"Hello."

"I was wondering when you would answer."

It was him.

Peter.

It's hard to explain how getting attention from anybody can brighten your day when you're in a dark space. But just him looking at me or thinking of me did surgery to my soul.

I wasn't just some "thing".

I was a person.

And that made me feel good.

Tye sat the diary face down. "Finally some real nigga shit!" He exclaimed as he walked into the kitchen and filled his glass with ice followed by Hennessy. "My bitch got a whole real ass nigga and she don't even realize how good she got it!" He said loud enough to be heard in the bedroom where Joanne was still pouting.

Flopping back on the sofa, he finished where he left off.

"Hey." I smiled so hard my cheeks hurt. That's really a thing. If you aren't used to smiling, it hurts when you do, especially if you smile for a long time.

I wish I had something else to say but that was the only thing that came to mind. At the time anyway.

"What you doing tonight?"

I sat up straight in bed. Did I hear him correctly? "Nothing."

"Sure about that? Sounds like you're having a party over there to me."

I almost forgot where I was. "I'm not having a party. My cousins are."

"Well let me come scoop you. Get you something to eat. Something that won't fuck up that gut since you sensitive and all."

I giggled. "Okay."

"You're easy-going. I like that."

"Why?"

"Females these days are too complex. And I like my woman to go with the flow."

I heard him blow out a puff of smoke. He was a weed head for sure. And if I got a chance to be around him more, I'm sure I would be one day too if I wasn't careful.

At the same time, his stuff always smelled off.

Like he laced it with something bad for the mind and soul.

"I don't know if I'm easy going or just don't have a life. The only thing I can say right now is that going out with you will make my day."

"Well then..."

He was still talking when suddenly my door opened and my cousin Penny walked inside. The moment I saw her face and eyes rest upon me I started crying. We used to talk for hours about any, and everything. So seeing her at my door holding a plate of food made me want to double over.

Was I forgiven?

"Why aren't you at the party?" She closed the door and walked over. I took it from her even though I wasn't hungry.

"I was giving you your space." I pushed the receiver into my bed, afraid she would say something he would hear.

She chuckled once.

I sat the plate on my end table and moved closer to her. "Penny, I really am so sorry about Greg. I'm sorry that I did that to you. But you must understand that it wasn't what it looked like."

"It was exactly what it looked like. Sex with my boyfriend is sex with my boyfriend. No matter how you label it."

"But...but it was The Crying Game. Did Nicole tell you?"

She chuckled again and I wished she'd stop.

"Did she tell you?" I repeated, feeling my entire body trembling as I waited for an answer.

"No she didn't."

I looked down. Nicole had never been known for getting someone else out of trouble but this was too much. She was ruining my social life. "I would have never gone there had I known it would hurt you."

"You and I have always been close. What about me makes you believe that I would want something like that?"

I thought about what she was saying. Had I thought about it before I would have never gotten into the situation in the first place. "I really was trying to help, Penny. I swear."

"I don't know if what you're telling me is true. That Nicole ordered The Crying Game on Greg. But even if she did you were never supposed to go through with it. You're smarter than that, even though you're more trusting than other people."

She was right.

"Will you ever forgive me?"

"What you're asking is unfair to me." She looked at me and then walked toward the opposite side of my room. "Forgiveness is earned."

Suddenly I wish I hadn't asked the question.

"Does that mean no?"

"Yes." She spoke.

I swallowed the lump in my throat. "Yes you will forgive me or yes you will never trust me?"

"I'm saying yes I hear you. And that's all I can offer you for now." She moved toward the door. "Eat up." She walked out.

And for some reason that was enough for me.

When I looked down, I saw the handset still in my hand.

Raising it to my ear, it was completely silent.

"Hello."

"I'm still here."

I smiled.

CHAPTER SIX
KINKY SALT AND PEPPER

T ye walked the last plastic chest of fresh vegetables into the kitchen of his restaurant.

His business was closed but he and his partner were setting up for later. When suddenly he had a pang in his stomach that caused him to lean on one of the stoves. When the gas dial turned on accidentally, instead of cutting it off, he looked down at it. Since it was an industrial stove, the fumes grew quickly. Slowly he bent down, preparing to take a deep breath when Logan, his best friend and business partner, walked inside.

"Nigga, what you doing? Trying to kill us?" He laughed, turned it off and slapped him hard on the shoulder. "I mean I knew you were getting scared but we can't turn back now. We in this shit for life."

"I'm not overwhelmed."

"I was just joking. Ain't nobody thinking you really getting high. I–."

"Nah, you said what you meant." He walked over to the sink. "You think just because we got a legal business it's too much for me."

He frowned. "I would never think that shit about you." He chuckled once. "Why would I go into business with somebody who I think can't handle it? But you have been looking out of it lately."

"So now I'm your bitch?"

Logan paused and crossed his hands in front of him. "You know that's the problem right there." He pointed in his face. "Men can't express emotions without somebody thinking it's deeper. At the end of the day, I just want you to know we good. And I got you. The Lit is and will continue to be a success."

"I can handle it."

"Fair enough." He raised both hands in the air. "Now what's going on? Outside of this business. Be real with me."

"Man...me and Joanne."

He shrugged. "What about it?"

"She pressing me about this wedding and shit."

He pointed in his face. "She should press you! Because I told you it would be too much. But nah...you wanted to marry *the love of your life*," he threw air quotes up. "And open a business at the same time." He laughed and began to place the fresh vegetables in the fridge. "Maybe in the future you'll start to believe me."

"She pulling me down. When we got married, I thought...I thought..."

"She could help more financially?"

"Yeah." He said honestly. "I mean she is a Davenport."

"Well she likes certain things. True. Some women are like that. At the end of the day what you're experiencing ain't new to any nigga who is about to get married. Maybe all it is are doubts."

"I want to talk to you about something but I don't want jokes."

Logan closed the refrigerator. "Then don't tell me."

"That's why I don't fuck with you sometimes. Everything is showtime."

"Relax!"

"I'm serious."

Logan stopped packing and leaned against the refrigerator while crossing his arms over his chest. "Okay. You got the floor. No jokes. I'm listening for real."

"I found this diary."

"Okay. Is it your little sister's or something?"

His jaw twitched. "No. It was this female's I met the night of our grand opening party. At least I thought it was hers but now as I continue to read it, I'm starting to believe it's somebody else's."

"Okay and what's the problem?"

"I don't know who it is and I gotta know. I scanned it looking for a name but then stopped."

"Why?"

"Because I realized that no one writes their own name in their diary." He paused. "The thing is...I don't know...like the chick in it is green and I...I..."

"Wait, you feel bad for her?"

"I didn't say that."

"You got a whole female at home pressing you about a wedding and you thinking about another bitch?"

"You know what... fuck it."

Logan laughed harder. "Yeah, aight."

"I'm about to leave and–."

"Go read your little diary?" He laughed so much his stomach hurt. Tye was almost out the door when he said, "Oh, before you roll, somebody came here looking at our spot the other day. He had all these tattoos on his face and shit. More than you."

Tye frowned and turned to face him. "What...what was he doing?"

"For real, nothing. He was just leaning against his car and looking at our spot through the windows."

"So! Did you say anything to him?"

"What was I gonna say? He wasn't bothering me. But he did have a gas container in his passenger seat. Almost like he wanted me to see it." He shrugged. "But maybe I'm tripping."

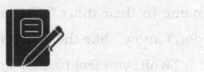

What Logan said played on Tye's mind. He knew it was Run but there was nothing he could do at the time. He would have to find a way to get the money or else.

For the moment, Tye was getting his car detailed while sitting in the waiting room. He was starting to believe that doing petty errands was just an excuse to put his head into the diary.

He didn't care though.

For some reason, the book was an escape he willingly took.

****

February 29, 2008, 8:14 PM
Dear Diary,

They didn't know I was home hiding in my closet.

Mainly because I was supposed to be at work and was too embarrassed to let them know what happened. That after Penny caught me with Greg, I was so depressed that I started calling out.

During the other days I just stayed up under Peter.

So they fired me.

I didn't care.

I liked him more than I was willing to let on. He saw the best in me even when I didn't see it myself. But he also brought out the worst in me too. Like I drink more when I'm with him. I smoked more too, but I don't like the way it makes my mouth taste.

I still think the good things about him outweigh the bad but maybe it's just me.

Anyway, when I heard Nicole and her best friend Lala talk about stealing money from Penny, my jaw dropped.

92

So I listened harder and tried to stay as quiet as possible to get the details.

"I'ma pay her back," I heard Nicole say. "Especially since you sounding like the police. Talking about it's wrong and shit."

"Girl, you can do what you want. I'm just reminding you that rent due in a couple of days. And using that girl's money to pay your car note is–."

"Shut the fuck up."

"You know what, I'm gone."

"Wait!" Nicole yelled.

I listened harder. I didn't hear the door close but I knew something was happening.

"What, Nicole?"

"I'll think of something to pay her back."

"Good...but whatever you do, leave me out of it."

I heard the door close.

When they left, I wanted out of the house. Last thing I needed was whatever Nicole was doing falling back on me.

But I didn't know where to go.

Peter was doing something he couldn't take me with him on so he was out. And with Penny being mad at me, I didn't want to spend time at home either if she walked in and gave me the quiet treatment. Since I didn't have a car I decided to go to the one place I went when I wanted to get over things.

The wreckage.

That's where I went to dance.

It was a building used by a local hair product manufacturer back in the day. Before a scandal, the co-owner killed her partner to gain 100% of the business. It was a shame too. That location employed a lot of people in the Baltimore area before things went sour.

I don't know why no one bought the building yet. Because despite the dust, broken windows from vandals and the overall creepy feeling which I chose to ignore, it was beautiful to me.

There were painted murals of women of all shapes and colors throughout. As a matter of fact my favorite place to go was on the lower floor towards the back of the building. There was a room with a mural of a girl who looks just like me.

Not the ugly me.

But the me I would be if I looked like what I felt like when I was dancing. Yep, it's my favorite room. I especially like how on the opposite side there was a wall covered with mirrors so I could watch myself move.

Say what you want about me but I knew when it came to dancing no one could touch me. I was flawless. I was light on my feet. It was almost as if someone more talented and confident than me took over my body when I danced.

At one time I gave myself the impression that I could make something of this talent. But Diary, I know in my heart getting paid to dance is a far-fetched dream. That doesn't happen to girls like me.

But I could be a star in the moment if I pretended.

So I turned my iPod on and played the playlist I selected for moments like this. With my headphones on, I tucked the device in a case on my hip, walked over to the mirror and allowed my arms to go high towards the sky. This let me stretch every area of my body at once. Then I swayed my arms from left to right up towards the middle and then down to the ground.

I stretched my legs one by one too.

Allowed my toes to flutter.

And then I began to dance.

The song slowly forced me into a rhythm I didn't want to do at the time. It felt angry. Bitter and afraid. But it also gave me strength. Before long, my body tingled from head to toe.

I remembered that it felt so good to have this skill. I considered it to be a superpower.

Maybe it was.

I was almost done when they entered.

Two men.

One dark skinned with kinky salt and pepper hair splattered throughout his face. The other could be white or Hispanic. I couldn't tell. And just like his partner their clothing was covered with so much dirt it looked stiff from where I stood.

Now the song that I love so much would act as a backdrop to what I knew was about to happen.

I was about to be raped.

And there was nothing I could do about it.

CHAPTER SEVEN
CHILDHOOD QUESTIONS

Sitting on the floor of his empty old apartment, Tye was just getting ready to learn what happened to the ugly girl when suddenly the door opened. He jumped up and was shocked to see his best friend, Logan.

"What you doing in here, man?" Logan questioned as he approached him. "I thought you gave this joint up."

"Nigga, I went home and tried to talk to her but she still beefing. I got tired of trying to get her to talk to me so I dipped. Needed some space."

"I don't believe she's the only reason you tucked in here hiding and shit." He moved closer. The diary was sitting next to him on the floor. "Is that the book you were telling me about? Because if it is, I'm even more confused on why you hiding to read it."

Silence.

"Tye, is that the diary?"

"If I say yes, then what?"

"What are we eight years old?"

"I mean you busting in my crib, coming at me hard so I want to know why you so interested now?" He shrugged.

"I'm coming at you hard because we were supposed to meet with the liquor board tonight. And I couldn't find you. I mean, do you even want this business anymore?"

"Stop sounding stupid. We just opened."

"I'm sounding stupid?" He pointed at himself. "You're sitting on the floor in an empty apartment that you were supposed to get rid of months ago reading a diary written by a complete stranger."

"You acting like I broke the law or somethin'."

"You're being irresponsible. And I'm waiting for an answer to make sense out of all this shit. Because it's off."

"You know I want the business."

"Actually, I don't."

"Just because you don't see things the way you want doesn't make them untrue. I just feel like something is up with this girl in this diary and that possibly I can help her or something. Maybe give her back her shit."

Logan dragged his hands down his face. "You don't even realize what you got, and it's crazy as fuck."

Silence.

"Tye, you dating a Davenport."

"Why do you keep saying that shit?"

"Because it's true, man. You have on your arm the most beautiful woman in the state of Maryland. And yet you reading the Diary of a bitch you said was ugly from the gate. Add to that the fact that you missed a very important meeting that's gonna cost us money."

"Her being a Davenport don't matter to me."

He chuckled once. "Except it does. Joanne being a Davenport is exactly what you needed to get shit done in Baltimore. She increases your worth. Remember? You already said that. And now you trying to sabotage everything."

"Listen, man. I get all that. And when I get some time to think about how to handle her, I'll do just that. But something is going on with this girl." He picked up the diary. "Yes I know that I don't know her. That much is true. But I feel like she may be in some sort of danger."

"Since I've been knowing you I've never seen you care about anybody but yourself. Definitely not a bitch."

"So you disrespecting now?"

He raised his hands, palms in Tye's direction. "I'm just stating the facts."

"If that's the case why be in business with me?"

"Because I accept you for who you are. The same selfish ass nigga you were since we lived in them fucked up ass projects. But I need to know right here and right now what you want to do with this business. Because I'm not about to waste any more of my time."

The truth was, Tye didn't know what he wanted.

Prior to finding the diary and reading the pages he felt he had all the answers. But something about the woman had him rethinking what he felt was important.

At the same time Logan was right. He was being very selfish. So what was it about the ugly girl that had him so interested?

It was a question he was trying to understand.

"Look, you're right. I been off lately. But I will meet with you for the liquor board. Just set the shit up again."

"Are you serious?"

"If I said I will, I will."

"You got to forgive me but your reputation is coming up short these days."

"I can only tell you what I'm telling you now. And I said I will be there. Schedule the meeting and I'm coming."

Logan breathed deeply. "Good. And go see about your fiancé."

"That doesn't have anything to do with you."

"So we not friends no more? I mean I know we got this business but..."

"Again with the childish questions."

"I'm saying that because a true friend will let you know when you're about to ruin everything. And I don't want that for you. So if I were you I would go see about my fiancé. Make sure shit's good."

"Maybe you're right."

"I know I'm right. I just want you to act on it."

He took a deep breath. "I'll go to the house in thirty minutes, Logan. Now get off my dick."

Logan laughed. "Cool, you want me to throw that diary in the trash on my way out?"

"Get out of here, man." He laughed.

Logan chuckled once and walked out the door.

The moment he was certain he was gone he rose. Walking to the window he looked outside.

Maybe he was about to destroy everything.

Maybe Logan was right.

So he grabbed his keys and even the diary and left out the door.

Little did he know, Run was watching from afar.

CHAPTER EIGHT
RUMBLE

Tye prepared a meal of Joanne's favorites.

Filet Mignon, rare of course. Au gratin potatoes with lemon butter and fluffy biscuits. To let her know he was sorry, he also chilled a glass of her favorite wine. Everything was perfect, and he made it that way.

So when she walked through the door, she couldn't believe her eyes.

Placing her purse down on the table next to the door she said, "Wow, I didn't know you would be home."

"If it's not me then who?"

Her mouth went up on one side in a weak smile. It was meant to be a joke but she didn't take it that way. "It's just that I wasn't expecting you to be home that's all. Kind of shocked me."

"I know and I'm sorry about my behavior lately." He placed the spoon down that he used to stir the lemon butter and walked over to her. "But in my defense I tried to talk to you and you weren't receptive."

"What is really going on with you these days, Tye?"

He thought about Run. "A lot."

"I need more." She said looking into his eyes. "There has never been a relationship I wanted more than this one and yet it has made me the unhappiest I've ever been."

"So you aren't happy with a nigga?" He stood over top of her. "That's what you telling me?"

"Should I be?" She looked up at him.

"I don't expect you to be through the roof every time you see me but to be the unhappiest in your life. I mean how you think that makes a nigga feel?"

"You want the truth right?"

"I'm serious, Joanne."

"And so am I. It seems like ever since you launched your business, you and I have grown further apart. And my father is concerned."

His eyes widened and he took one step back. "So you...so you told him about our relationship after I asked you not to?"

"I tell my daddy everything. You know that."

He glared. "I know you used to do it when we first got together. But in my opinion what goes on between a man and his woman is just that. Between a man and his woman."

"Well I didn't have anybody else to turn to."

"What about them cackling bitches you keep time with?"

"Cackling?"

"Most females hit up their best friends first. But you go to your father?" He yelled. "You act like it's been this way for months! Prior to a couple of days ago things been going smoothly between us! Or is it just me?"

She looked down. "No. It hasn't been this way always."

"So why you making it sound like it is? And to your father at that." He dragged both hands down his face. "Fuck, Joanne!"

"I'm just afraid, Tye."

"Afraid about what?" He threw his hands up in the air before allowing them to slam down at his sides. "It ain't like you in this bitch getting raped!"

"What the fuck?"

"I mean what you afraid about?" He yelled louder.

"That you won't want me."

"There is no woman I want more in the world than you."

"Are you sure about that?"

For some reason he thought about the woman in the diary. A woman who was unattractive. A woman who he'd never met. And a woman who despite all that shit, lived in his mind rent free.

Was he feeling her too?

"I'm positive."

"You know what...I don't wanna fight no more."

"You sure?"

Slowly he eased down on his knees. She was wearing a dress which was perfect for what he was about to do next. Sliding her red panties to the side he slipped his tongue into her warm pussy.

She moaned. "Ty...Tye...don't..."

"Don't tell me don't, girl. This my pussy right?"

She trembled in delight.

"Answer me." His words made her pussy lips rumble.

"Yes...it's your...it's your pussy."

"I know it is."

Back in focus mode, he slipped his tongue deeper into her before sliding it out and gliding back and forth over her clit. She was feeling so good she knew she was about to explode in his mouth.

"Tye, I don't wanna cum like this. I want to feel you."

He heard her pleas, but the thing is he wanted her to bust early. Because if she was satisfied, he would be free to do whatever he desired afterwards. So he flipped his tongue faster and more firmly.

Before he knew it she had exploded in his mouth.

Rising up, he wrapped his arms around her waist and pulled her closer. "That thing stays sweet."

"What has gotten into you?" She breathed heavily, with a look of satisfaction on her face. "I can feel your passion."

"Nothing. But I know what's about to be into you."

When she felt his throbbing stiff dick pressing against her belly she knew what he wanted. "I...I don't know if I have...if I have the energy to..."

"You crazy if you think I'm not gonna fuck this pussy. You wet too."

Before she could kick back with excuses, he lifted her up and took her to the bedroom. Lying her down on her back on top of their mattress, he slid her closer. Her legs hung off the bed as he removed her panties fully.

Pushing down his boxers he lowered his height and slipped into her. Slowly he allowed his muscular body to press into her warmth, until his dick was covered with her juices. Rising up methodically, he pushed in and out as he looked down at her beautiful face. During moments like this he was reminded of how bad she was.

The way she bit the corner of her bottom lip when they made love always sent him over the edge. This time, however, he thought about the unknown girl from the diary. He wondered what it would be like to fuck her too.

He wondered how she would feel as he eased with precision in and out of her pussy until she was calling his name.

He wondered about the ugly girl.

Closing his eyes, his mind was so filled with thoughts of her, that before long, he exploded into Joanne's body. And when he looked down at her, he could tell she had done the same.

"That was...that was...nice." She said, as her breast rose and fell.

He winked, eased out of her, and grabbed several pieces of tissue from the dispenser on the dresser. "Is that right?"

"But where did your mind go?" She curled up in a fetal position. "When you closed your eyes? I had a feeling that I lost you for the moment."

He was caught. "On how good your pussy tasted. And how sexy you look."

She smiled. "And yet you didn't even say anything about my hair."

"What are you talking a..." He saw it now. Her brown hair had been slightly reddened. "I didn't...I didn't..."

"Notice." She grinned.

The oversight fucked him up. "It looks good on you though."

"I'm...I'm glad you like it." She winked, running her toes over his chest. "But...well...I..." a yawn escaped her lips.

"You good?"

"I'm perfect now."

"Tomorrow I figure we can go grab something to eat and...you know, I'll show you a good time. Shit been crazy but I want us to do a reset. If you want."

He could see the exhaustion and excitement on her face. "I want that too." She paused. "But tonight...you mind if...if..."

"You take a nap?" He chuckled once. This was always his plan.

"Yes...I'm just wiped out." She begged with her eyes for him not to be mad.

Her endurance in the bedroom was always trash so this was on brand. "Nah, I'll put dinner up so you can have it when you get up." He snatched his robe and moved toward the door. "Get some rest."

"And Tye?"

He stopped. "Yes?"

"I...I fucking love you."

He winked and walked out the door.

After turning off the stove, he grabbed the diary hiding behind another book on his shelf. Something about the way his books were set up seemed off, but he figured she must've dusted.

Flopping on the sofa, he reopened the diary.

CHAPTER NINE
PERKS

****

March 3, 2008, 9:20 PM

Dear Diary,

I almost didn't write this entry. But I write everything that happens to me.

Good and mostly bad.

So why wouldn't I write how...how they...they made me dance first.

The black one with the salt and pepper kinky hair said I had pretty legs and pretty arms to match. The other one stayed quiet and watched me move stiffly. Not like water like I had done before.

At first I thought the Hispanic one disapproved of how his friend looked at me. I didn't know his age but I knew he was much older. But after a while the truth came out. He wasn't looking because he didn't like what his friend was doing. He was looking at me in silence because he couldn't wait for whatever happened next.

The black one went first.

He was rough and heavy on my body. I remember thinking that he was much heavier than I'd think a man his size could be. He penetrated me from the front and he smelled of urine, spoiled food, and dirt.

I wanted it to be over.

Quickly.

The other one went next.

He was meaner. Crueler. And took the flat of his hand to push down on my face as he moved in my body. His eyes closed and he was quick, rough, and angry.

They did almost everything they could to me. And now as I write this entry I wonder how I didn't blackout. How I kept my mind steady.

When they were done, the black one crashed my iPod by throwing it and stepping on it with his bare foot.

I couldn't even have my music.

Why do these types of things happen to me, Diary?

Do you know?

Later on that day I walked out into the middle of the street and called Peter from a phone booth. At first he didn't want to come

112

because he claimed something was going on with him on his end. I didn't fuss too much because that's not in my nature. But there must have been something he heard in my voice because as I was walking down the street, he pulled up in his car.

He unlocked the door.

I slipped inside.

"You look dirty."

I nodded because I was.

His car smelled of weed and a chemical I knew was designed to destroy his mind.

"What were you doing here?" He asked looking at the wreckage behind me.

Should I tell him the truth?

I decided against it.

"I dance here sometimes."

He frowned. "Why would you dance in a neighborhood like this?"

"Because it's private."

At least I thought that way before they found me at my most vulnerable.

"You're weird." He opened his glove compartment and pulled out another blunt. "You want any?"

I shook my head no. Something I've done several times before when he asked.

"Well you look like you could use some. And I want you to have it."

He was probably right. After all I was just raped.

Would it help me forget?

"Maybe just a little."

He smiled. Like he finally was able to get me to do something I didn't want to do. Maybe I'm just making stuff up. Maybe I'm just trying to fill the pages of my diary. But I got the impression that after saying no so long that saying yes had him feeling like he won.

Won what?

I don't know. I never considered myself to be a prize.

He lit it for me. I inhaled and quickly spit out the nasty flavored clouds. It tasted exactly how it smelled. Danky. Chemically. It didn't leave a fresh odor on my tongue the way I would have preferred.

But after a while I suddenly felt better.

But not the better I normally did if I was tired and was about to get into bed. I felt weighty. Heavy. Like my body was being pulled down to my seat even though I was already sitting.

"I want you to be my girl."

I was already his girl whether he knew it or not. I told anybody that would ask. And since I didn't have any friends I was mostly talking to myself.

I nodded. "Okay."

"Did you hear me?"

"Yes."

He frowned. "Are you going to open your mouth?"

It wasn't until that time that I realized I hadn't been nodding. And I hadn't been speaking even though I thought I was. Instead I was stuck off the drug.

"Yes. I want to be your girl."

He grinned. "Are you happy about it?"

I nodded yes.

"Let me hear you say you're happy."

"I am happy to be your girlfriend. I've never been anybody's girlfriend before. So you saying that I'm yours does make me feel good."

"Do you know what it means to be somebody's girl?"

I didn't.

So I shook my head no.

"It means you have to do whatever I ask when I ask."

"Okay well is there something from me you want now?"

He looked like he was thinking about it long and hard.

I waited.

Because I was willing to do anything. It didn't matter what it was. As long as he didn't leave me and that I was able to call him my boyfriend, to me nothing else mattered.

"Not right now. But I want you to remember this in the future. Girls sometimes forget what they say when they lonely."

"You think I'm lonely?"

"Yes." He smiled. "It's all in your eyes."

Since he decided he was my boyfriend I wanted to tell him what happened to me in the building. Not that I wanted him to do anything about it. Besides I thought the men may have been long gone anyway. But it just needed to come off my heart. Instead of occupying the spaces in my mind and the pages of my diary.

"Something happened to me today."

He pulled over and looked at me. I remember thinking that was sweet. "For real?"

"I want to tell you but I don't know how you will react."

He grew serious. "Well before you tell me let's break it down."

"Break it down?"

"Do you think this thing you are going to tell me will make me look at you differently?"

I thought about the things they did to me and said, "Yes."

"Okay. Do you think the thing you are going to tell me will make me not trust you?"

Again I thought about what he asked. It was stupid, now that I think about it, to go to the warehouse without letting anybody know I was there. And again I said, "Yes."

"Is it worth telling me this knowing that I could think differently about you and not be willing to trust you?"

It wasn't worth it to me. I never said the words but my expression must have done the job.

"Since I said you my girl I want to start all over from scratch. Let the past stay in the past before you entered this car. Know that I won't hold anything against you because I didn't know you then. And that nothing matters more than where we go from today."

For some reason even though I didn't get a chance to release, I did feel better. Maybe it was because I know I have you, Diary.

Or maybe it was because he saved me. Because had I told him and he did look at me differently I would have felt extremely alone. So, by knowing in advance that he thought so deeply about everything, it's like I dodged the bullet.

"Are you hungry?" He spoke.

There are a lot of perks to having a boyfriend. But being asked if you want something to eat, to me, is on the top of my list.

"Yeah."

"Let me take you to get something to eat."

"Where?"

"Anyplace you want." He turned the car on and pulled off.

"I would like that."

"Good, cuz after that I want you to make me feel good. And do whatever I ask."

"What you mean?"

"I'ma pull over and let you suck my dick. Can you do that for me?"

I did.

CHAPTER TEN
BITTER

Tye's mother was fist fighting his sister when he pulled up.

He didn't have time for any of it, seeing as though he was supposed to be meeting his best friend at the bar to speak to the liquor board. Not only that, but later on that night, he was supposed to meet his fiancé at their favorite 5-star restaurant.

But he wasn't doing any of that shit. Instead he was being forced to deal with his mother and sister once again. As he drove and parked in the parking lot of their building, he saw them wrecking.

This was something he'd seen before, but this time shit was worse when he saw that his little sister had a knife and she was coming at his mother full speed.

"What you doing, Ava?" He yelled jumping out of the car, leaving it half open. "Put that shit down!"

"Tye!" He heard a loud male's voice say calmly.

When he looked behind himself he saw his father Oliver sitting in a car which was odd. Ever since he'd known his father he always, always rode his motorcycle except on the rare occasions it snowed. He even rode in the rain.

At the moment he was drinking a forty and looked busted.

"Fuck are you doing here?"

"I'm watching my girls." He took a large sip. "To make sure it don't go too far."

"Watching! Nigga, what?"

Oliver laughed.

Tye waved the air and rushed over to Ava. He slapped the knife out of her hand and pointed toward the building. "Go the fuck in the house!"

"But daddy told me to defend myself!"

"Against your mother?"

"Yes! He said–."

"Ava, get in the house before I drop you! Now!"

"I hate you!" Crying like a mad woman, she ran upstairs.

Quickly he walked over to his mother. "Are you okay?" He touched her battered lip.

"Just get off of me, Tye!" She sobbed. "You don't care." She looked at her ex and back at him. "You don't care about nobody but yourself." She picked her purse up off the ground. "If you coming in the house, Oliver, I'll be back in five minutes. I'm going to get some air." She walked off.

Tye was livid.

He was mad because his mother called him and then acted like she didn't want him there since Oliver was around. And he was mad to be looking at his father, even though he hadn't seen him in months. He was just about to get in his own ride when his father walked up.

"What you doing, boy?"

Tye continued toward the car.

Oliver grabbed his arm and slammed his car door shut. "Didn't you hear me when I said I had them? I wasn't gonna let them kill each other."

He snatched away. "Fuck you even doing around here? Huh?"

He looked at him and laughed. "You so bitter to be so young."

"It ain't about being bitter. It's about you coming around here, fucking with ma's head when you know you don't give a fuck about her."

"That's my woman."

"Was your woman!" He stepped up. "Stay the fuck away from here."

He glared. "And if I don't?"

"You heard me right?" Tye threatened.

122

Oliver laughed. "The only thing I heard is that you had better get over the past to make room for the future. Or it will be taken from you."

Tye walked to his car and pulled off.

Tye was on his fourth drink as he sat at his favorite bar thinking about his father and his mother. It fucked him up that after so many years, he still had control over his mother. He wished she was stronger because when he was in the picture, shit got worse.

But she wasn't.

And there was nothing he could do about it.

"Fuck is up with you, Tye!" Logan yelled, slipping next to him at the bar. "Just tell me the truth."

The moment he saw him he drove his hand down his face. He was a victim to his habits and so Logan always knew where he roamed. "Look, man. I'm sorry about the liquor board. My mother called me, I go over there and she fighting Ava. While my father standing by and–."

"You always got a fucking excuse. Why?"

"Excuse? Did you hear what I just said?"

"You had me set that meeting up with the liquor board and again you didn't show up. After you promised me you would."

"Didn't you hear when I said my mother and–."

"And your sister. I know, I know!" He said sarcastically. "It's always them. And I'm tired of this reality tv show shit."

Tye was done.

Turning his body toward him he said, "Who the fuck are you talking to anyway? You ain't my bitch."

"And it's a good thing I'm not either. Considering how you treat her."

"Fuck you saying?"

"I went over there, Tye. To find you for this meeting. And once again she was crying."

"You know, you seem to be awfully concerned with my bitch these days. You got something you wanna tell me?"

"Yeah, get your shit together otherwise everything you worked hard to build will be gone. This is my final warning." He took his drink off the bar, drank it all, slammed it on the counter and stormed out.

CHAPTER ELEVEN
FLAGELLATION

Tye left the bar bent.

He knew he had too much to drink, but everything seemed to be crashing down around his once perfect world.

Like with Joanne.

Just when he thought he convinced his woman that shit would be good, after fucking her right, he failed to take her out for the dinner date he'd promised due to dealing with his mother and sister yet again.

It was his idea at that.

Not even hers!

In addition, he pretty much said fuck you to Logan and the liquor board which pushed him further from the spot he needed to pay Run's debt.

Lowkey he felt like saying fuck it.

Fuck Joanne.

Fuck the liquor board.

And fuck Logan.

He was in the alley next to his bar thinking about his life as these thoughts rolled through his mind. Although he was not sober, he figured going

126

inside would remind him about everything he was building. Maybe if he saw his new restaurant, and appreciated his dream coming true, then maybe he could stop wasting time.

His hand was on the handle to push himself out of his car when his phone rang. As he rocked and moaned, trying to locate the gadget, he lightly patted his pocket once and found it stuffed inside.

Slipping it out, it threatened to fall from his grasp due to being lit, but he placed it lightly against his ear. "H...hello."

"You hate me."

It was his mother.

"What you want?"

"Son, I know you're mad at me. I asked you to come over only for your father to be here too. And I'm sorry. I wish I could be a better mother. But I'm not. I am the mother you got."

He sat back, looked up and shook his head.

"But just because your sister is getting her period, don't mean she should be talking to me any kind of way."

"Wait, what the fuck are you talking about? You go straight from an apology to whatever you got going on with Ava. Ma, what you want from me 'cause I'm not in the mood?"

"I want you not to be so fucking judgmental."

"I'm still waiting on why you called. And why you called that nigga when you know he don't give a fuck?" He moaned, as the scent of his alcohol binge filled the car. "I don't get it."

"I know you don't care much for your father. But have you ever wanted a person so badly that under any conditions you'd be willing to see them?"

"Nah."

"Well I have."

"He sat in the car and watched you fight your daughter barefoot in the parking lot. His daughter at that. Had I not pulled up, he would've let her stab you for entertainment. And that's what you want?"

"Son, I–."

"Is that what you fucking want?"

"I want...I want to be...I want you to find my–."

"Don't say it."

"Tye, you have to address it."

"Not here. Not now."

He hung up and the moment he prepared his drunken body to exit his car, Clark Davenport, Joanne's father, slipped inside and locked the doors.

When Tye looked out the window, he saw four other Davenports too. Including Joanne's brother Chris.

Clark was a large light skinned man with thick black hair and thick eyebrows. Although he was on paper as one of the premiere real estate moguls and the father to some of the most beautiful women in the world, including Joanne, at his heart he was a killer.

"What's going on with you?" Clark placed his thick hands in his lap, which were calloused from fights from the past.

"I don't understand the question."

"What are you doing to my daughter?"

He sighed. Once again Joanne must've gone crying to him and he hated that about her. "I mean, I thought we were good. What she tell you?"

"You aren't good. And as I made clear to you before, I don't like my daughter crying over niggas. I don't like my daughter upset."

"I didn't make her upset. I just missed a date out for dinner. I mean why is this such a big deal? Couples fight all the time."

"Not if one of the members of that couple is a Davenport." He pointed at his face. "And my daughter is a part of this couple right?"

Tye wasn't sure because for real he wanted to be done with her ass after this shit.

Clark rolled the window down and Chris handed him a long object, the size of a sword, tucked inside a leather case. "Have you heard of the act of flagellation?"

Suddenly Tye's car door opened. "No...I..." He was pulled out and thrown on the ground by one of Clark's clan members.

Clark exited the car and slowly walked toward him. He removed the case off the object and showed him a *cat-o' nine tails*.

Tye frowned. "What is going on?"

"I don't know how much Joanne told you. But my family is originally from Afghanistan. And when I was living there, under the Shari's law, one could be flogged for adultery."

"Fuck that got to do with me?!"

The Davenport men immediately pinned him against the wall as Clark walked toward him. "And I am one hundred percent sure you cheated on your woman."

"I don't know what the fuck you–."

"The night of your party." He brought the whip down on his arm. "We know you were with another woman. In your car. There is no use in lying."

130

Tye was livid, but in that moment, he was too shocked to tell him so. He had been caught when he thought he was hidden in the alley. "I don't know what you talking about. I didn't–."

Clark smacked him on the right arm with the *cat o-nine tails.*

Now he felt the pain.

Every time he tried to deny that he cheated, Clark struck him with the whip again. In the end, he was left beaten and out of air.

"Were you unfaithful to my daughter the night you opened your restaurant?" Clark breathed heavily.

Beaten and confused, he said, "Yes."

"This goes against the vows."

Since everything was out in the open, Tye wanted to know more. "Did you, did you plant the diary in my car?"

Clark frowned and it was at that time that he realized he didn't. "What are you talking about, boy?"

Tye shook his head.

"Drop him." Clark demanded.

His body fell limp to the ground. And at that time Tye could see the marks on Clark's wrists that were welted. Had he experienced this sort of treatment too?

Maybe for pleasure?

"You will do right by my daughter." He pointed at him.

"We not even married yet." Tye said, mostly out of breath.

His head tilted. "What did you just say?"

"You hit me for adultery and I ain't marry her yet."

The Davenports laughed.

Clark didn't.

"Are you threatening to break my daughter's heart again? By calling off the wedding. I mean, is that something you really want to do?"

Silence.

"Answer me!"

"Well, I figured since you caught me cheating you would want it off. Maybe even tell Joanne."

"Nah. She doesn't know. And I want you to think carefully about fucking around on her in the future. Because I won't bring this next time." He raised the *cat o' nine tails* and dropped it to the ground. Slowly he lifted his shirt, revealing a .45 handgun. "I'll use this instead."

CHAPTER TWELVE
FRESH AIR

Tye carried several bags into his old apartment which included a blow-up bed, chips, juice, and a bottle of Hennessy. Also in the bags was a medical kit that he would need after dealing with Clark. And above all, he brought his most prized possession of the moment, the ugly girl's diary.

First he took a shower.

Then with the towel wrapped around his waist, he stood in front of the mirror to observe himself. The wounds Clark caused were still open and slightly bleeding, but for some reason he didn't feel much pain.

What the injuries did do, however, was make him despise his fiancé. He had heard stories of the Davenport women using their father to get what they wanted, but he never had to deal with this level of insanity. So what they didn't see eye to eye. He felt like getting her father involved because he didn't take her on a date, knowing he was a madman was too far.

134

Taking a deep breath, he opened the medical kit and dabbed alcohol on the open wounds. Then he put Neosporin on the gashes.

Once done, he slipped on a white t-shirt and some gray sweats before blowing up the mattress and pouring himself a drink. He was preparing to rip into the diary when his phone rang.

Unfortunately he answered. "What?"

"Tye."

It was Joanne.

He placed one hand behind his head and was lying face up looking at the white ceiling. The phone was pressed against his ear. "What do you want?"

"I'm...I'm sorry." She sniffled.

"For what part?"

"I didn't know he was going to come to you and–"

"What you mean you ain't know? I fucking told you about getting your family mixed in our shit. And what do you do? Involve him anyway."

"You did but–."

"I'm busy."

She sniffled. "Please...please don't hang up. I...I just wanna say that I don't want us to break up. I figure we can work this out if we try. I mean...I mean...I love being with you. I love spending time with you. And all I want to do is be your wife. Have your babies and make you happy."

"I can't get into that right now. You gotta give me some time."

"O...okay...I know you might not come home. But...but can you tell me when you will? That way I can be here so we can talk about–."

He hung up before she could finish. Besides, it had been hours since he dove into the diary. And he needed to find out what else was up with his girl.

More than anything he needed an escape.

****

March 14, 2008, 3:13 PM
Dear Diary,

We spend so much time together.

But something feels off.

I love being with Peter when he's happy. But secretly he has these moments of not being present. Mentally and physically.

It scares me.

136

When you're used to having nobody and then get somebody, the idea of losing them becomes scarier than any horror movie I can think of. I figure if he lets me in more, maybe I can learn to do things that will make him want to come around.

I want to know more about him. I need to know more about him.

So I decided to ask him about his life one night when he picked me up to get something to eat. The moment I slipped in his car I said, "Who are your parents?"

He chuckled once. "Why you wanna know about them?"

"I wanna know anything you wanna tell me."

He shook his head.

Did I annoy him already?

"For the most part they are childhood sweethearts. Still close to this day. Which is why I prefer being in a relationship."

"Then how come you never take me to where you live?"

"So you think I live with my parents?"

I really thought he did. He didn't deny it either. "Yes."

"I don't take you to my place because I prefer to take you out. I know you ain't used to having a boyfriend but girls prefer to be taken out."

"I get that...but I...I wanna know you. All of you."

We were in the far-right lane with another lane on the left. But when the light turned green he made a u turn which caused the car in that lane to almost hit us. But just like that we were going in the opposite direction.

"Where are we going?"

He didn't answer.

At the time, I didn't know if he was mad. I couldn't tell much of anything about him to be honest. All I know is that he was driving slowly but urgently at the same time.

It's hard to explain, Diary.

We were going somewhere and I knew our relationship was about to change.

After an hour we were outside of this large red brick building. It looked neat enough outside but at the same time, abandoned.

Strange.

When Tye's phone rang again he was annoyed.

At the moment nothing was more important than finding out what was happening in the diary.

Still, he picked it up without looking at the screen.

"Hello!"

"Wow, you sound like I disturbed you or something."

It was Run.

"What you want, man?"

He chuckled once. "You mean outside of my money?"

"I'm working on it."

"Make it quicker. I'm growing impatient with–."

He hung up.

The nigga was already after him. So why should he listen to him make threats on the side?

Instead, he reopened the diary.

We trudged into the brickhouse building and up a small, tiny hallway. I smelled pine which comforted me a little because it meant somebody cared.

In my mind anyway.

Walking up to apartment number nine he looked back at me and said, "Are you sure you want to get to know me?"

"Yes."

"Because it's not clean. I mean, I wasn't expecting company. We never do anymore. But you should be good right?"

We?

I nodded.

He opened the door and the moment he did I wanted to leave. This didn't smell like a dump. It was a dump. The odor of trash that had been sitting around too long felt everywhere. There were so many pieces of clothing on the floor that I couldn't see any furniture.

And then there was the floor.

There was debris in every place I looked.

I'm not talking about just empty containers. I'm talking about half eaten sandwiches. Cups with drinks in the corner. And when I looked down I could see ants making quite a living for themselves.

I kept brushing my arms to make sure I didn't get anything on me because it was that filthy. Finally we made it to his bedroom door and I was prepared for the worst.

I was shocked.

When he opened the door I saw that it was a totally different place. It was neat and despite the smell stemming from the outside, I saw incense in holders in various areas in the room. He lit one and opened the window which brought in noise and fresh air.

I welcomed both.

The bed was made, kind of stiff, and I sat down on the edge and watched him stuff a towel under the door.

"What's that for?"

"To keep out the bugs."

I nodded.

Why didn't he or whoever else lived there just clean up?

He grabbed the remote off the end table and pointed to a door off to the left. With a push of a button the TV blared.

"Go wash up."

"I can't hear you!"

He turned it down. "Go clean your ass and pussy." He opened his drawer and pulled out a pair of boxers and a white t-shirt. Both were neatly folded. "Put this on when you come out."

I quickly did as told because I still felt like bugs were on my skin.

I rushed inside, got undressed and turned on the shower.

When the water ran over my body, I remember feeling grateful for washing the men who had taken advantage of me off my skin again. I showered many times since that night but they stayed with me, always. And when I ran the sudsy washcloth between my legs, it still stung a little where they had ripped through my flesh.

I wish I could talk to him.

I wish I could tell him.

But he didn't want to know. I was sure of it now. He actually said let the past remain in the past.

After I was cleaned I came out and sat on the bed again. He walked past me with a folded set of clothing in his hand.

He went inside and showered too.

As he was gone I looked around the room and saw he smoked that stinky blunt again while I was inside. I'm glad he did it while I was in the bathroom because I didn't want another one.

Five minutes later, when he came out he seemed more relaxed.

His eyes were glassed over and he stood in front of me.

"Still glad you came over?"

I nodded yes.

"You're my girlfriend right?" He ran his knuckles softly on the left side of my face and raised my chin.

I nodded yes.

"Let me hear your voice."

"I'm yours."

"You don't love me."

"Love?"

"Do you love me or not?"

I looked around and then back up at him. "Yes...of course I do."

"You love me enough to be my slave?"

I looked down again. "Yes."

"Good, open your mouth."

I did.

He was already hard. And slowly he pushed himself into my mouth. He placed a warm hand on each side of my face and moved back and forth. I guess I wasn't doing much. Literally before he guided my head my jaw was just widened.

At least he was clean.

He made me suck. Long too.

My jaws hurt because it seemed like forever.

I didn't complain.

But the pain got worse.

I felt him holding back. Like he was dragging it out. So I finally got into it. Moaning. Wagging my tongue in the places I could move it. Finally after ten minutes I tasted his thick salt roll across my tongue and toward my throat.

I swallowed.

It wasn't half bad.

"You staying with me tonight." He pulled back the sheets and ordered me inside.

For some reason I smiled.

Tye jerked off as he reread the last pages of the diary entry.

Visualizing her being so submissive turned him on in every way imaginable. After he was done, he drifted off into a kink sleep.

CHAPTER THIRTEEN
LIC-HER-LIE-CENSE

Tye had just gotten out of the shower and was drying off when he heard a knock at the door in his personal apartment. Since outside of Logan, no one knew he still kept the apartment, he was confused on who was visiting.

Pushing the bathroom door open a bit wider, he walked slowly toward the front door, leaving wet footprints along the way. Inching to his peephole, he saw someone dressed in a black hoodie. Because the hood covered the person's face, he couldn't tell if they were male or female.

It didn't matter.

What the fuck did they want?

"Who is it?"

The person, whose head remained lowered, knocked again.

"I said who the fuck is it?"

"Open the door."

It was a man.

Suddenly Tye was upset that he didn't have his weapon. He had stopped carrying one many years ago due to being on paper. If the police ever caught him with one he would be sent to prison for life. "Who the fuck do you want?"

"Does Shaun live here?"

He breathed a short sigh of relief. "Nah. Now get the fuck from in front of my door."

The person remained standing.

"I said bounce!"

The stranger nodded and walked off.

Despite the "misunderstanding", he was certain that the person would be back again. And so he would have to consider new ways to protect himself.

Especially if that person worked for Run.

When Tye walked outside of his old apartment, he was surprised to see his mother was leaning against his car with a glare on her face. "You cut me off financially?"

Maybe Logan wasn't the only person who knew he still kept his old place.

"What you talking about?" He opened the back of his car and tossed in his book bag which included the diary. "And get off my ride."

"Son, why would you stop the payments to my account?"

He chuckled. "I'm sick of the freeloading ass shit."

"Freeloading? You know I have an issue with my back from when your sister was born. I can't work and–."

"And I got shit I gotta do with my restaurant. Ask Oliver's ass."

"That's not fair! And it doesn't matter what you have to do. I'm your mother. And you know I can't work right now."

"But you can drink?" He clasped his hands in front of himself.

"Wow."

"Let me tell you something, my finances have changed." He said firmly. "And even if they didn't, I'm not fucking with you no more."

"Son, I can't–."

"Until you learn to treat my little sister right and stay away from that nigga, I'm done."

"Your sister! Have you talked to her about her part in all this shit? She's the one who's being disrespectful. Not me!"

"SHE'S A FUCKING KID! WHEN ARE Y'ALL NIGGAS GONNA STOP THINKING JUST BECAUSE SOMEBODY WALKS, THEY CAN MAKE DECISIONS FOR THEMSELVES?"

Her eyes widened in fear. "You...you blame me for your upbringing?"

"I blame you and that nigga for putting decisions on our shoulders that we should've been left out of."

"Tye, please. I need the money. You could have at least told me you were–."

"I don't owe you shit!"

The sun hit his chain and blinded her for a second. "This gonna come back on you, son! And I don't want this for you!"

"Then let it come."

He walked around her, got in his car, and pulled off. He could see her buckling down crying from the rearview mirror, but he was done with the games. Done with the shenanigans.

Just done.

Tye walked into his restaurant to what could only be described as a heated scene.

His friend, Logan, was consoling an ugly twenty-four-year-old woman as her friends rubbed her back and stared at him with hate as he made his way inside. They knew him.

Everyone knew Tye Gates.

Tye had no idea what was going on, but he knew it wasn't good. "What's up?" He asked, walking up to them.

Logan sighed in relief. Looking at the women he said, "I'll be right back."

"Just do something!" One of the friends yelled before rubbing the crying friend's back again. "Cause this shit not right!"

Stepping out of ear shot from the ladies when they were some feet away Tye whispered. "What's going on? You finally disappointed one of your bitches in the bedroom?"

"This shit not funny!" He snapped.

"Fuck is your problem?"

"They paid for a party right after we opened. Complete with a catering package and everything."

"Okay?" Tye shrugged. "So what's the deal?"

"No...LIC-HER-LIE-CENSE, nigga."

Tye shook his head. It was all making sense and once again, to hear him tell it anyway, it was his fault. "Okay?"

"So they can't have a party if we can't serve drinks, Tye."

"So why would you accept the reservation in the first place?"

"Because a week before we opened, you assured me you would be there when the board wanted that meeting. And that everything would go through. But it's like you running from the police or something. And I want to let you know, whatever you trying to dodge won't go away."

Run entered his thoughts.

Tye took a deep breath and walked back over to the women. "My name is Tye Gates and I'm one of the owners."

"And?" The meanest friend said. "Fuck can we do with that information?"

He glared at her and focused back on the unattractive woman. "And I want your birthday party to be a success," he said, ignoring her friend.

150

"So I want to invite you to have your party here and we will provide all of the food for free."

Logan grabbed his arm and said, "Maybe we should talk about this before we do all of—."

Tye shook away from him and refocused on the birthday girl. "And we will make sure liquor is here that night too. On the house."

She sniffled. "Do you...do you promise?"

Tye placed his hand over his heart and raised his free hand. "You have my word."

"Now this is how you do business," she said to Logan. Looking back at Tye she said, "Thank you...thank you." She smiled and wiped the tears away before heading for the door.

The friends looked at Logan and rolled their eyes, before following behind her.

"What the fuck are you doing? Rescuing ugly bitch's on account of that diary?"

"You wrong." He pointed at him.

"NIGGA, YOU TRIPPIN'!" He paused. "In order for you to do something like that, it means you're holding back!" Logan said. "And I'm tired of the games! I need to know right here and right now what it is!"

Tye took a deep breath and walked toward the kitchen sink. Rolling up his sleeves he said, "I ain't hiding shit. I took care of it."

"No...what you did was put us in a bigger bind."

"Why do you care if we give them free food?" He turned on the water and pumped the soap. "The shit gonna be all over the Gram anyway. If anything more business will come right back to The Lit."

"Nigga, who are you?"

"Like I said, you said you were upset about the drama and I took care of it."

"How? We aren't even getting a coin from this shit. And a box of ugly bitches crowding in our restaurant ain't gonna do shit but get us closed! I need to know what is on your mind so I-."

"I got a record." Tye lathered his hand so much they were white. The bruises from the whips Clark caused began to sting.

Logan tilted his head, stepped back, and said, "Wait...what?"

"I said I got a record."

"A...a misdemeanor? From when you did that little drug time?"

He cut the water off and snatched several pieces of paper towels and dried his hands. "Nah."

"A felony?"

He tossed the crumbled paper towels in the trash, turned around and leaned against the sink. "Yeah, man. From moving weight back in the day."

Logan looked like his entire world was rocked. "So I went in on this spot with you, just for you to...just for you to..."

"I can still get a license."

"You can try! But we both know with a felony in the state of Maryland they'll look for any reason to deny you."

"It's gonna be alright. Calm down."

"So tell the truth, this is the other reason you got with Joanne. You thought she could help get you the license?"

"I thought she was gonna put up her name. But she didn't want to go in. So I chose you."

Hearing about the plan made Logan enraged. "That's why you asked me at the last minute."

"Yeah." He shrugged.

"You always plotting on niggas. Always doing what the fuck you want. One day that shit gonna hit you hard."

"I'm just telling you the truth."

"Do you even love that girl?"

Silence.

"You know what...if we can't get that license I'm done with this business and I'm done with you too." Logan stormed out.

Just then his phone dinged and it was Joanne on the other side he glared at the message.

Tye are you still gonna marry me?

CHAPTER FOURTEEN
STRAWBERRY

Tye sat outside of the apartment he shared with Joanne for one hour. He knew she was inside because her car was out front. But he didn't feel like going in. Something about being with her at that moment felt dry.

So he drove the fuck off.

Instead of returning to his old apartment, he went to a hotel, tapped his credit card for a room and got himself situated.

After checking in, first he cleaned his wounds, then he poured himself another drink, downed it and did it four more times. When it was all said and done, he was five drinks in and lying on the bed when he reopened the diary.

****

March 23, 2008, 5:35 PM

Dear Diary,

Today I saw my aunt.
She looks bad.

As I'm writing these words I don't know how to feel. I expected it to be such a happy moment, because even though my aunt and I are close, up until that day she had always lived out of town.

If she hadn't we would be closer. I wouldn't have as much bad karma.

Because she and I got one another.

She would always say she was as weird as me.

I think it was true.

The day started out easy going in her new apartment. I had gone over to her house happily after she told me she would make my favorite meal.

It's simple, Diary.

I love fried chicken, collard greens and mac and cheese.

But there's something about food that's made with love that tastes so good. I didn't want to be a freeloader. So I brought over strawberry cake which she loved and we ate in her small kitchen and talked about everything under the sun.

We talked about her boyfriend who would be moving down in a few weeks.

We talked about her job and how it was so easy she could do it in her sleep. She even suggested that I apply since all she had to do was answer phone calls from home. And then I reminded her how nervous I am to talk to most people.

She didn't say much after that. Just told me that I could do anything I set my mind to once I got ready.

We talked about my boyfriend Peter. And how I liked him so much. And how he put a smile on my face even when he didn't know.

Even if he wasn't around.

When I was sitting in her kitchen just thinking about spending time with him later, it got me excited in a way I didn't think I would ever feel.

I liked to say I was in crazy love.

We also talked about mama.

Although I didn't like to talk about mama too much. It's not like I didn't love her. But there is a special kind of emptiness in a person's heart when their mama is no longer on Earth.

I know about that emptiness.

I can almost handle anything.

But when she died, half of my reason for living died too.

My aunt must've realized talking about my mama was too painful. So she decided we should talk about something else. I agreed until I realized what that something else was.

"I'm dying."

I didn't get it.

What does she mean she was dying?

"I don't understand."

"You heard me, Strawberry."

She called me that sometimes and I always liked it because it meant it was our little thing. But today it didn't feel good.

"I said I'm dying."

She repeated it as if it was as simple as sitting across from her with half-eaten food between us. As simple as the air which flowed from the vent directly above our heads. As simple as the smell of fried chicken which still wafted in the kitchen and would remain on my clothes all day.

This wasn't a simple thing.

This hurt.

Badly.

"But why do you wanna leave me? Why are you dying?"

The words may have sounded selfish, but they were how I felt.

"Do you remember me asking you to get a mammogram last year even though you were young?"

I nodded yes.

"I said it because I knew at that time that I would be dying from the same thing your mama died from. I said it because I had already gotten my mammogram and they also saw the tumors. I said it because I didn't want you to worry before I told you that I also have cancer."

The room was spinning.

Literally.

I looked up one day what causes a room to feel like it's spinning when you are scared or nervous. I found out at that time that it was vertigo. It's normally a symptom of something else worse happening, but I got it now.

I was losing the only person who truly loved me.

"I can't let you go. I'm not ready."

"I knew you were going to say that. So check this out, I want you to move in with me. I came

159

back here so we can spend my last days together. I want you to know how much you meant to your mama. I want to tell you all the stories she told me about how much she loved you. I even wanna tell you about your father and his people, so you can maybe build a relationship with them. And so that when you're a mama, you can put that love into your child."

I can't be nobody's mama.

Ever.

"You know where they are? My father's side?"

"I do. Took some time but I found them after learning about the cancer. When your mother first got pregnant with you she thought your father was her boyfriend. She loved that man so much she wanted you to be his. But after a while it became clear that it was not him. Instead, your daddy is your mother's first love."

"I don't want to meet him. I want you to live."

I begged her like dying was her decision.

But I knew it wasn't.

And then she gave me a gift I still appreciate to this day.

160

"You still dancing at that old, wrecked building?"

The thoughts of the rape entered my mind. I looked down in shame. "No."

"Good, cause there's a new dance studio in town. A friend of mine will let you use it as much as you want. For free. I want you to go there now and get rid of some of the pain you probably feel in your heart. And then I want you to come back and return to me."

"Where is it?"

"Off Reisterstown Road. Near the Hilton."

I looked down on the address she gave me. The dance studio was called The Falcon.

Suddenly I couldn't see her clearly. My eyes were covered in tears. The gift was so thoughtful. So wrapped in love.

I felt unworthy.

"Strawberry, you will be..."

I wish I could remember what else she said. I can't.

Because I passed out.

CHAPTER FIFTEEN
THE RAVEN

Tye had just finished getting his car detailed when his little sister hit him up on the phone. He had plans later but he figured he'd hear what she had to say. Besides, they may have gotten on his nerves, but when it came to her he had a weak spot.

"What you want?" He asked, sliding back in his car. "Because if you fighting with ma, y'all can leave me out of that shit."

"I think I'm pregnant."

He felt gut punched. "What you mean? I told you to stop fucking with that old ass nigga who–."

"It's not by him."

He glared. "Then who you pregnant by?"

She giggled.

"Who, Ava?"

"One of daddy's friends."

Tye saw black. "Where are you?"

"At Tracy's Cornerstone."

Within ten minutes Tye was in front of Tracy's Cornerstone. It was a building for social media influencers. She liked to hang out there because it

162

was colorful on the inside, but on the outside, in the alley on the right, was a huge mural of beautiful black women with colorful hair and clothing.

Tye quickly rushed her as she was talking to two of her friends.

Grabbing her by the arm he pulled her a few feet away and said, "What the fuck are you talking about you pregnant by one of Oliver's biker friends?"

She smiled and sipped her frosty ice drink. "I just told you. I'm with child." She rubbed her belly.

"Why you fucking some old ass man?"

"He's not that old. He's eighteen and daddy don't know yet so shut up."

"*Daddy don't know so shut up.* Are you insane?" He knocked his knuckles against her forehead.

"We sneak around sometimes and–."

"You can't be having nobody's baby, Ava! You a kid yourself. A stupid ass one at that."

She laughed.

"Fuck is so funny?"

"You should talk about babies." She giggled.

He glared and stepped back. "You know what, I'm done with you and ma."

The smile wiped off her face. "Why?"

"Why?" He said sarcastically. "Because you and ma must like all this hot shit. And I don't have time for it no more. So don't hit my phone." He walked toward his car.

"You gonna hit me before I hit you. Trust and believe."

"Yeah, aight." He pulled off.

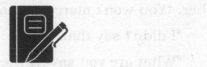

Tye was sitting on the sofa when Joanne walked inside.

She placed her purse on the table and crossed her arms over her chest. "What you doing here?"

"What am I doing here?" He sat an arm on the back of the sofa, crossed his legs ankle to knee and sat back.

"Yeah. What are you doing here? You ain't been here in days, Tye. So don't act like I'm crazy for my question."

"I live here."

"Do you though?"

"Sit down." He patted the seat next to him.

"I don't want to."

164

"I'm serious."

Finally she took a seat to his right. The moment she saw his arms and the bruises she went off. "Oh my God what happened to..." she stopped talking. She knew what happened now. "My father did...he...do this?"

"I'm good."

She turned forward and looked out ahead of her. "You won't marry me now will you?"

"I didn't say that."

"What are you saying then?"

"I think we rushing into stuff, bae. I really do. And to be honest, this is all on me. And I'm sorry about it."

Her eyes widened. "You told me you wanted me to be your wife. You said–."

"I know what I said."

"So what changed?"

"I got a lot to think about. I got to work on me. There is a lot of things you don't know that I haven't shared with you. It's–."

"Ever since you got a hold of that diary you have changed."

He glared. "What you talking about?"

"I see you around here with it, Tye. Holding it like it's your bible. Taking it in the bathroom with you. I'm not stupid."

"You never saw me with that diary. Ever. I made sure of it. Now tell me this, Joanne, how did you know about it? You had something to do with me getting it to fuck with my mind?"

She stood up and made herself a drink. "Does it matter who told me how you be treating it like it's the Quran? I'm your–."

"Logan." He shook his head.

She looked at him. "I didn't say that."

"Did he tell you about it or not?"

"What you need to know is this, you promised to marry me. And you are going to marry me. Because if you don't, then...well." She took a big sip. "I hope your wounds continue to heal before my daddy get at you again."

The diary sat in the passenger seat as Tye looked for The Falcon dance studio. Try as he may, he could not find a similar name anywhere. At this point the diary had consumed him and he wanted to learn more about the ugly girl. He didn't want to wait any longer.

To be honest, he wanted to see her in person. To judge for himself.

It wasn't like she was drop dead gorgeous, to hear her tell it. Like Logan said repeatedly, she called herself unattractive. And at the same time he didn't care.

Was he falling in love with a stranger?

Nah...

Couldn't be. He thought.

Although he couldn't find The Falcon, he did manage to find a strip club in the area he believed the studio would have been. The moment he parked; he sat in his car for a second.

Was the dance studio she talked about actually a strip club? And more importantly, what was he really doing there?

He decided to park and go into the small danky spot that by all accounts was empty. Afterall, it was a little early.

Walking to the back, he sat at a round table set up for two. In the center of the dark club a lonely girl danced on the pole for a crowd of four which included him. A single bill rested at her feet but she didn't seem to notice.

Or care.

"Can I take your order?" A skinny white girl wearing a too small pink bikini asked.

"What you got?"

She seemed to lighten up. "Whatever you want." She said, pulling her bikini strap upward with her thumb, revealing an unbudded titty.

Any other day he would be in the back of that spot with his dick in her mouth. But tonight he wasn't in the mood. "Nah. I'm good."

She glared. "Then what you drinking then? 'Cause you can't be in here using our wifi and wasting my time."

"Hennessy on the rocks."

She stormed away and he saw that she was actually barefoot. Feet as black as a turned off iPhone screen.

"The fuck?" He shook his head and continued to watch the dancer who was doing a poor ass job of performing. Instead, she kept taking what could only be described as invisible seats in a chair on every area of the stage.

"Ain't you Tye?" A dancer said walking up to him.

She was cute, dressed in all purple. Her skin was chocolate and her eyes were doe like and innocent even though he knew she wasn't. This clashed against her body which rocked nicely in all the right places in the tight bodycon dress she wore.

"Who asking?"

She giggled. "My name is Light."

"Light?"

She nodded. "Yep. And where I'm from you a hood legend."

He appreciated the compliment but didn't feel like unsolicited company. "Thank you." He turned around and looked at the dancer who was now on the stage, sitting ass flat while fixing the buckle on her shoe. Her pussy fell lazily out of the bikini bottom she wore.

"What brings you in a place like this?" Light asked.

Just then the white girl slid his drink so hard across the table it almost fell off the other side. Luckily Light caught it. "That bitch." She spoke, as she stormed away.

He took the drink. "What's her problem?"

"She just be mad she gotta work in the daytime and don't nobody tip her or use her services. They may do it if she put on some shoes and wash her nasty feet."

He nodded.

Suddenly he thought about something. "How long you been working here?"

"Why? You about to Pretty Woman me?"

He chuckled. "Nah."

"Oh that's right. You with a Davenport."

He glared. Shawty was alright until she mentioned her name. "How you know that?"

"Everybody knows you with her. Now what's your question?"

Suddenly he wasn't in the mood but proceeded with caution. "How long you been working here?"

"Oh, that's right. You did ask me that. For as long as I can remember. Since I was eighteen."

She didn't look older than that now but then again, she was black. "How old are you now?"

She laughed. "Yeah, aight. I never tell my age or my price until the time is right."

He nodded. "What was the name of this spot? Before it changed."

"Speedy's Point."

"Not the current name. The older name."

"Oh, it was The Raven."

His eyes squinted. "Not The Falcon?"

"Nope. Both are bird names though so maybe it's the same thing right?"

Hearing her call the place The Raven instead of The Falcon had him for the first time doubting that everything in the diary was true. He believed for the most part the author was being honest, after all, why lie?

But he never stopped until that moment to think that there could be some possible deceit behind the words.

"Was this a dance studio?"

"Back then?"

He nodded yes.

Not sure but I do know it wasn't a strip club. Like I said, I wasn't working here back then but I believe it was some kind of workout gym or something like that. It didn't go over well once the big named gyms started opening up though. But from what I hear it was here for a long time. Why you asking so many questions about that? You trying to work out?"

He paid for the drink he didn't touch by dropping a $20 bill and placing the stained glass on top of it. Next he gave her a $20 bill and walked toward the door.

"You sure you don't want nothing for this? Like a lap dance or somethin'? I mean, I wouldn't mind. It would be like a favor if you want to know the truth."

He winked and walked out.

The moment he approached his car he saw Run standing next to his silver Benz.

Maybe he should've taken the lap dance anyway, especially if he was about to be killed. Maybe he should've let ole black foot suck his dick too.

All hindsight was twenty-twenty at that moment.

Run was glaring and looking his way. And before Tye could enter his vehicle he was grabbed and beaten within every inch of his life.

CHAPTER SIXTEEN
TOOTHBRUSH

When Tye woke up, he was in a hospital bed. Surrounded by so many flowers he thought he was witnessing his own funeral. Confused, he raised his head trying to see through the balloons because he couldn't understand what was happening.

Then he remembered.

He encountered Run.

How bad am I? He thought.

And where is that diary?

Realizing that he had to adopt the first things first mentality, he decided to check on the damage to his body. Looking downward he took a deep breath and wiggled his toes.

They worked.

Next he took his right leg and bent it slowly.

It worked.

He did the same to his left and still all appeared to be in working order. With confidence he raised his hands, arms and even wiggled his head. The relief came because at that moment he was certain that no matter how badly Run had injured him, he didn't paralyze him for life.

For the moment anyway.

Now where was that diary?

Suddenly the door opened and in walked Joanne, Clark, and his son. Didn't she remember that it was over. If he had to think of the last people on Earth he'd wanted to see at that moment it would definitely be them. And yet there they stood in his hospital room taking up too much space.

Joanne, playing the dutiful fiancé rushed to his bedside, sat down, and grabbed his hand a bit too roughly. "Are you okay? Can I get you anything?"

He was too annoyed to speak. Even if she wanted to see him, which was cool, why bring her father and brother? At the end of the day he wondered what they were doing there.

"No, I'm fine." He tried to wiggle his hand away but she gripped harder.

"You don't look fine." Clark said walking closer to the bed before bumping it just a little bit with his physique. "It looks like you got yourself into trouble. Again. What is it about you that the worst always seems to happen?"

Tye looked down at his arms with the whelps still visually apparent and glared. "I'd like to be alone."

Clark nodded. He figured he wasn't in the mood to see him as of yet. Considering how he whipped him before this event and all. "I'll leave you with your fiancé. But you have to take care of yourself if this wedding is going to go through with you alive."

"You gonna force me to marry her if I'm dead too?"

Clark glared.

He started to wonder why they were so interested in him marrying her. Did he have some kind of strange insurance policy on his head that he didn't know about? After a few seconds going over possible scenarios it came down to one thing.

Although she was beautiful, she was needy.

And more than it all, she belonged to a family that would scare the average man. This would explain why despite her beauty, she remained single. No man that valued his life would ever be with her. Not with her gangster father threatening every part of their relationship.

Why hadn't he seen it before?

Oh, that's right.

He didn't want to see.

He needed her name.

Not only that...he also loved her beauty. How she tasted, felt, and even smelled. In the beginning Joanne was highly submissive. Possibly making up for the danger she knew was lurking from behind with her family. Of course there were other beautiful Davenports in their lineage. But they were all married and each of their husbands were stressed out.

Seriously...

You could see the wrinkles on their foreheads.

The bags that dressed their eyes due to limited sleep and stress.

These women were sirens. Put here to destroy men to hear Tye tell the story.

And he was stuck with the last Davenport available.

When his future father-in-law and his son left the room Joanne squeezed his hand harder. "You can't scare me like that, Tye. I almost died when I thought I lost you. I mean, who hurt you like this?"

The way she spoke as if her family wasn't capable of much more irritated him. "It doesn't matter."

"You're right. I'm just happy you survived."

"Me too."

She released his hand. "Tye, would you agree that a lot has been going on since you opened your restaurant?"

"I do."

"And would you agree that if we just tried we could be happier?"

He didn't. But he said, "I hear you."

"So what do you need from me?" She grabbed his hand. "To make things easier. I don't care what it is, I think you should ask me now."

Tye took a deep breath. He didn't know what she had access to but he wondered if she could get her hands on one hundred thousand dollars. "I need money."

Her face tightened in a lifeless smile and she clamped down on his hand a little harder. "Okay."

"One hundred thousand dollars. Can you give me that?"

"Tye...I..."

"It's okay if you don't have it."

"I never said I didn't have it." She grinned.

A sudden weight lifted off his shoulders. "Good."

"I'm just not gonna give it to you."

He frowned. "So you got the paper but I can't have it?"

"I'm doing you a favor. You wouldn't want to start our marriage with owing that much money." She giggled. "Why do you need it?"

"It doesn't matter."

"Fair enough." She grinned. "So, let me tell you what I need."

He could care less since his needs weren't met. "I want that diary."

He frowned. She already was forcing him into a relationship he wanted out of and now moved like she had the money to save his life but wouldn't give it to him. So he wanted her gone. "Why?"

"Because it's causing us problems." She smiled. "Where is it?"

"I don't know."

"I'll look for it myself. But I want you to know this...we are going to make this work. You'll see." She released her grip on his hand. "The Lit will continue to do numbers too and get you out of whatever debt you're into. Watch! I have faith!"

The moment she left he scanned the room. He remembered that he brought a small bookbag with him the night Run got to him. He had plans to make a few recipes with noodles and cheese sauce

178

he dreamed up at The Lit. So he bought his composition book and a few spices to work on them later at his restaurant.

The diary was in there.

Sitting up straight, he tried to see past the flowers in his room.

Then he spotted his bag.

He grinned.

There was a problem. The more he moved his body, the more he experienced pain that caused the monitors to alert the nurse that his blood pressure was rising. There would be no way he could walk in that condition. A pretty light skin girl with hazel eyes rushed inside.

"Oh, no..." she gently nudged him back to the bed. "You can't do that. You suffered an injury to your head."

He heard her but he had one request. "Can you get me something for the pain?"

She frowned. "Medicine? Because on your record, it says that you had an addiction at one point."

He sighed. "I know. But I haven't taken anything in years. Outside of liquor."

"Technically you shouldn't be doing that either but–."

"Please. The painkillers. This shit hurts."

"Okay. I'll see what I can do. Anything else?"

"Yes. Hand me the diary in that book bag over there."

****

April 1, 2008, 7:37 PM

Dear Diary,

I hadn't seen my auntie in over a week.

She calls but I'm not ready to have the conversation. I'm not ready to talk about what it would mean to see her die. I did that before. I watched my mother go from two hundred healthy pounds to under a hundred before she closed her eyes.

I'm not ready to live with my aunt, and not be able to get a full night's sleep without putting a mirror under her nose to make sure she's still alive.

Why would she ask me to do this?

Why would she ask me to move in with her?

I feel like it's selfish.

Mean.

I thought she loved me.

The good news is that I got a new job. One that is inside a building with controlled air conditioning that's in a safe area. It pays more money too and I don't have to see people. It's in a warehouse.

So Peter and I celebrated although he never really looks at me.

Mentally he's out of it more than ever.

But he still spends a lot of time with me. The kind of time where two people exist in the same space, even if they barely say a word to one another.

And then I made a mistake.

I always make mistakes.

Maybe I'm just bad luck.

"Sir, did you want something to eat?" The brown eyed nurse said entering Tye's room, irritating the fuck out of him in the process.

He closed the diary briefly.

"Listen, I don't want nobody else to come in here, okay? Especially a nigga with more tats on his neck than me."

"I'm sorry," she raised a tiny pill cup. "I brought your medicine though."

He took it from her, downed it without water and said, "You can leave now."

She looked at him, shook her head and walked out.

When she was gone he reopened the diary.

Maybe I'm just bad luck.

But I decided to spend a couple of nights at Peter's so I wanted to take some clothing with me. And I invited him inside our apartment.

The moment I opened the door and saw Nicole and Lala I regretted my decision.

"You still live here?" Nicole asked. She was talking to me but looking at my boyfriend.

"I'm just coming to get some clothes. Staying over my boyfriend's house tonight." I looked back at Peter.

"Your dry ass love saying 'boyfriend' huh? Like somebody cares."

I didn't respond. Just looked at Peter and said, "Come on."

He followed me, but I saw him give Nicole a look. Didn't know what it meant but I hoped it meant he didn't like her either.

Diary, I never packed so fast in my life. I was about to grab my toothpaste when Nicole and

182

Lala slid in the room and leaned against the wall across from my bed.

"So why you like my cousin?" Nicole asked him. "You cute."

"Fuck that supposed to mean?" He spoke.

"Uhh...I just told you." She was chewing a piece of gum which she grabbed a bit of to pull out of her mouth, leaving a trail from her fingertip to her lips.

"I like what I like." He spoke. "What difference does it make? Ain't nobody come to see you."

She frowned. "Yuck."

"Why you gotta act all smart to my friend?" Lala said to him.

The way Peter ripped into her inspired me. "Can y'all get out of my room please?" I snapped.

Nicole looked at Lala and they both busted out laughing. "This bitch must be getting some good dick because she tripping now. Acting like she won't get knocked out if I move across this room."

Things went too far. "I want privacy."

"Like you wanted privacy when you fucked your cousin's man." Nicole said.

My heart dropped.

"Sucked his dick and everything," Lala said, talking to me but looking at Peter. She wanted him to dump me, I could tell.

I felt the room spinning.

I didn't look at Peter but I could feel him gazing at me.

"You made me do it."

"How can I control your pussy? Or my bad, your throat." Nicole said, tossing the gum back into her mouth before chewing like a cow. "I'm just a little old–."

"I hate you." I didn't know where it came from but it sure felt true. "And I hope you die."

Nicole glared. And for some reason, it looked like for the first time ever I hurt her feelings. "Bitch I don't give a fuck about–."

"Whether she fucked dude or not, you shouldn't be putting your cousin out there like that. Didn't you hear her say I'm her nigga?"

"I was just–."

"Get the fuck up out my girl room."

Nicole was stuck.

"Now."

They rolled their eyes and stormed out, slamming the door behind themselves.

184

When they were gone, I left so fast I knew I forgot things. But I was afraid of what would happen next if I stayed. When I was in the car I realized I left my toothbrush.

Once outside, we sat in silence.

And I was scared. Scared he wouldn't want me anymore.

So I reached over and touched his hand to check his temperature.

He looked at me, shook his head and pulled away.

CHAPTER SEVENTEEN
TEXAS

Tye was still in the hospital bed.

When he woke up, he saw Joanne reading the diary. His stomach dropped. Shooting up from the seated position he said, "What are you doing? Why you going through my shit?"

It wasn't until that moment that he saw that she had a soft grin on her face. It was as if she was reading the diary and thought the whole thing was a joke.

Comedy even.

Since he had a different view on it as he read the diary he didn't understand her reaction. But he didn't need a review either.

"I asked you a question. What you doing reading my book?"

She looked up at him. "Book? So you are a girl writing a diary now?"

He adjusted the sheets over him. "You know what I mean."

"Actually I don't." She cleared her throat, looked down and mocked the words. "*This is an ugly girl's diary. Don't bother telling me it ain't true*

cause I won't believe you. My eyes are too far apart.
My weight ain't been steady since my mama–"

"Fuck is wrong with you?"

She closed the diary but it remained in her lap. "Why you walking around reading this thing? Logan told me you had it but–"

"So it was Logan."

"For starters you stopped taking his calls regularly. At one point you stopped taking mine. And I needed to find out where you were. So who better to ask than your best friend?"

"I don't understand why this is an issue for both of you. What I do ain't got nothing to do with y'all."

"True. When he first told me you had this thing I thought I had something to be worried about. But the chick in the book said she's unattractive."

"So."

"So?" She repeated before raising her arms and looking down at herself. "I mean, look at me. I'm a star."

For the first time ever he was starting to see that although she embodied the only thing he cared about, good looks, that was all she was worth. "If you so confident, why worry about somebody busted in that diary?"

"Tye, you have been carrying this book around for days. And I could be wrong but I believe you have been isolating yourself just to read it. So if you don't care about her please tell me what the fuck is going on because I'm confused. And honestly, starting to have a fucking complex!"

"This wedding is off. I kinda told you that before but it's official now."

A slow glare crept on her face. "What did you just say?"

"You heard me."

"I have ordered a dress. We have paid for the hall. And caterers. You will marry me, Tye."

"We're talking about a lifetime. Not an event. I don't want to marry you."

"Well I don't accept." She smiled. "You told me you could see being with me forever. So I'ma need you to make that happen unless you're dead. I want babies. I want a future. And I want it with you."

"I don't love you anymore."

She blinked her eyes several times. "I...I don't care." She paused. "Love can be taught. Learned."

Slowly she rose and the diary fell to the floor, irritating him even more. His eyes remained on it, even though she was standing at his bedside holding his hand.

It was like he was obsessed.

"Who do you need me to be, Tye? More submissive? Aggressive? Demanding? I can be a version of everything you want. Like an avatar." She nodded. "As long as you keep your promise. Because...because–."

"I'm not giving you another script. You failed. And so I'm not marrying you, Jo. I don't know how else to say it."

She squeezed his hand and then let go, before allowing her nails to scratch him when she dragged it away. "Do you wanna die?"

"What?"

"I asked, do you wanna die?"

Silence.

"Because I can oblige if you want."

He shook his head. "Wow."

"My father literally asked me earlier today if I was sure that you could love me." She ran a finger down the fabric of the sheet. "Was I sure that you would do right by me. And I said yes. Because I don't want him to hurt you."

"He already did."

"Imagine what else he could do."

189

He was so angry he chuckled.

"I'm serious. Think about it, Tye."

"It doesn't even matter."

"People always say that until it does."

"At this point, like I said, he's gonna do what he's gonna do. And I'm good with that."

The brown eyed nurse walked in with another pill. "Oh, excuse me. Didn't know you had a visitor."

Joanne rolled her eyes at her.

The nurse cleared her throat. "Sir, I was told to give you another in four hours if need be."

"Thank you."

Joanne's eyes suddenly widened. "I get it now. You're taking drugs again. That explains why you don't understand who I am anymore. So I'm going to wait until you leave the hospital and when you're prepared to act right, I will be here waiting." She left.

He took the cup, downed the pill, and said, "Thought I said no visitors."

"I'm not a guard."

It was true.

"Can you give me that book off the floor?"

She picked it up and handed it to him. "Are you sure you're okay?"

190

He thought about the question. "I'm in a situation that I didn't see coming. And for some reason I don't care. So the answer is yes. I'm fine. For now." He opened the diary and continued to read.

****

April 6, 2008, 2:15 AM

Dear Diary,

I haven't heard from Peter since I left his apartment for the weekend. After Nicole told him about Greg.

Even when I was there, in his bed, I felt like he wanted to be someplace else.

Why do I always get the heartaches?

What is it about me that's so damn unlovable?

I'm starting to not care about anything anymore.

And I don't want to be that way.

I want to believe in love so badly my skin itches.

At least the job I have turned out to be okay. The people there are nice and I get the

191

impression that they want me to like being there. And I want to like being there too.

I just can't stop thinking about Peter.

****
April 20, 2008, 9:30 PM
Dear Diary,

Peter came over yesterday.

I asked him where he'd been and he told me he couldn't remember. I was just happy that he came back around so I didn't fight with him.

I know there will come a time when I must fight with him though.

When I must fight with everyone.

When I must fight with myself too.

Just not right now.

I always wondered why I stopped feeling real emotions. Or feeling a way about things happening to me. And then I remembered it was after my mother died. When you lose your mother, and it's unexpected, even though I watched her die, you learn that nothing is promised.

And since that's true, I wonder why so many people make promises they can't keep. They like saying things they don't mean. Things that are meant to keep people in line.

Really they're just lies.

I don't need stories anymore. Just tell me the truth. I prefer things that way.

Anyway, Peter didn't come over to make excuses. He didn't come over to make promises. He came over to have sex with me.

"Pull down your panties and bend over." He told me.

I did.

He pushed in and out of me like I was some foosball table in the middle of a basement floor. Still, it felt good. Contact with another human when you're lonely always feels good.

At least it does to me.

****

April 26, 2008, 2:30 PM

Dear Diary,

My aunt called me today. She said she needed to see me. I agreed to go over tomorrow. But I don't want to.

Please, God.

Don't make me.

****

April 28, 2008, 6:00 PM
Dear Diary,

I went to see my aunt today.

She looked bad.

Despite having lost weight, she still managed to find the time to make my favorite meal. I didn't even have the energy to eat it. Instead I messed around the plate, pushing things to the left and right to give the illusion that I was chewing.

But she knows me.

She knows me better than anybody else.

"Are you moving in?" She asked.

I smiled.

Then she said the words I couldn't come back from. "I need you, Strawberry. I can't get around without feeling winded."

I blinked rapidly.

"Things are getting harder, and, well, I broke up with my boyfriend."

"Why?" My lip trembled. Prior to then, I was comforted in my absence that at least he was helping. I guess I was wrong.

194

"Because I want this time for you. For us. Will you move in?"

"Yes. I will."

I could feel huge tears roll down my cheeks. Like by saying I would move in that it would be a death sentence for her or something.

"Don't look at it like a bad thing," she reached over and touched my hand. "We're going to have fun. Trust me. And then when it's time, I'll go into hospice so you won't have to see my final days."

"Hospice?"

I hadn't heard about hospice until that moment. I didn't know there were places that could take care of the people who were dying. What kind of human could work in a place like that? Is it possible to see death so much that you become used to it?

I certainly wouldn't want to work in a place like that.

I certainly wouldn't want to be subject to that kind of pain.

"Okay, Strawberry?"

I smiled. "I'll be here for you, auntie. But I want to be honest. There will be days where I don't feel much like being happy. Are you going to be able to understand that? Because I was afraid to cry in front of mama. I will allow myself to cry in front of you."

"I can take as good as I can give."

I think she meant it too.

****

May 3, 2008, 3:30 PM

Dear Diary,

Yesterday I packed all of my clothing. I was ready to live with my aunt.

And then something happened that I hadn't expected. Penny walked up to me as I placed the last of my items into my box.

She was so pretty.

Did I say that before?

"Can I talk to you for a minute?"

I sat down on my bed as the answer.

She sat next to me. "So you really are moving?"

I couldn't speak. How could I? Every time I saw her I thought about The Crying Game. Yes it was stupid but it stayed on my mind most of the time. Like it did at that minute.

"Yes. To take care of auntie."

"I want to tell you that I'm sorry."

I frowned when I wanted to cry. "I...I don't understand."

"Last night I came home early from work and overheard Nicole talking to Lala. They were drunk as usual. You know how they are when they get that Hennessy up in them."

I laughed even though I didn't see anything funny. I hated when they were drunk. Because they always used the time to fuck with me.

"Anyway, they were talking about The Crying Game. And how you so easily fell for it. How she made you eat mayonnaise and so many other things on the marble counter in the kitchen."

I was embarrassed by that part.

"Even though I wished you were stronger to see the game she was playing, I also know what kind of person you are. You're sweet. But you're also smart. People don't know that about you. But I do."

I didn't believe her. "I don't know about all that. I'm-."

"It's true. You have patience. The kind of patience that will pay off in the long run. I only wish I was like you."

Tears scrolled down my cheeks.

"At the end of the day, I know you did what you did with Greg for me. I know you thought you were helping me. The crazy part about it is you were right. By exposing what kind of nigga he was I realized I had no business being with him in the first place."

I took a deep breath. "So what's going on with you now?"

"I'm moving too."

"Where?"

"Texas. A friend of mine just bought a new house. And it's one of those two-family homes that gives her more space than what she needs. I figure I'll stay with her for a little while until I can get on my feet."

"I think that'll be good for you. But I will miss you. A bunch."

"The same." She looked down and I could tell she wanted to cry. I just wasn't sure why. "Listen, I want you to start fighting for yourself."

"I don't understand."

"Except you do."

I swallowed the lump in my throat.

"The kind of fight you need doesn't have to be violent. Although I'm sure if you aren't careful, the things you have gone through may come out in an explosive way. And I'm afraid. So start taking up for yourself, bit by bit. Piece by piece. To prevent that from happening."

I nodded.

"Promise me you will think about what I'm saying."

"I do. And I will."

"Good." She got up, grabbed my phone, and stored her number. "I put my new address and cell number in your phone. Call me whenever you need to. Even if it's just to talk."

She moved out the same day.

I used the number too.

Because the next day, my auntie died.

CHAPTER EIGHTEEN
FUMBLED

The doctors told Tye that he would need to stay in the hospital two more days, but he made a turn for the better. The moment he got out of the hospital, the first place he went was back to the strip club. The same one he had been hit outside of that landed him in the emergency room.

This time Light was his bartender and he was happy because she was the person he was coming to see.

"Hey," she smiled. "Nice seeing your fine ass again."

He nodded. "What happened to the other girl? The white one." He sat down.

"Oh, she got fired for being rude."

"I wish I could say I'm surprised."

"Not me." She waved the air. "She got on my nerves. She got on everybody's nerves to be honest." She took a deep breath. "So how are you? After the assault."

"You know about that?"

"Everybody does. Did you know the guy? That hit you."

He didn't feel like going into detail about his story. If he didn't tell the police who visited him regularly, he damn sure wasn't going to tell a stranger. Besides, he was there to see her for other reasons.

"You mentioned this place was probably called The Raven before."

She nodded yes.

"Do you know anybody that worked here at that time?"

Her eyes went up and then down. "You mind if I have a seat?"

"No."

She took a deep breath and joined him. "There was a cook who worked here at that time. I believe he was doing some kind of janitorial work then. But when it became a strip club he stayed on. He's the only person I can think of."

He sat up straight. "Do you have his address?"

"Can you at least buy me a drink?"

He reached into his pocket and laid $100 on the table. "You can keep the drink. I just want anything that you can tell me to lead me to the truth."

Tye pulled up at the diner off of Liberty Road. The moment he parked he could see a man smoking on the side of the alley. This man fit the exact description of the one she gave.

Long graying dreads and thick black eyebrows dressed his face.

He parked his car, got out and approached Dreads.

"You got an extra one?" He really didn't want it but he was trying to ease the tension that occurred from a stranger walking up to another.

"No. Sorry." The way he glared Tye knew he wasn't.

"I heard you used to work at The Raven."

"Who's asking? The IRS?"

He chuckled. "I'm actually looking for a girl."

"I don't go like that. You better go down Rt. 40 if you want pussy. I ain't–."

"No...not a girl in that way. She used to dance there."

He glared. "The Raven wasn't a strip club back then. It was something like a gym."

"I'm informed. But...but I'm talking about somebody who may have danced there for fun. Maybe she was with a dude."

"I need more."

It wasn't until that point that he realized that nowhere in the diary did she indicate that Peter ever went with her. Maybe she was a loner. Maybe she came there on a regular basis.

"She may have had a tattoo. Strawberries."

He smiled. "I see tattoos all the time. But, the only person that I remember who fit the description was a real cute girl about 5'6 or 5'7 I believe. Out of everybody that enjoyed the gym, she was broken down the most when she learned it was closing."

His heartbeat thumped in his chest.

It had to be her.

Although the person writing the diary said she was ugly was it possible that once again there was some deceit to uncover?

"So she was, she was attractive?"

"Beautiful. I got the impression that she didn't know. Which made her even more attractive. But she would dance around that studio like she had wings."

"Do you know her name? Maybe have a picture?"

"No. I don't."

His chest deflated. "Okay."

"Do you know what happened to her?"

"From what I've been told she definitely hit a hard patch. People used to speak about the things that happened to her. I heard so many different stories I can't remember one that's worth repeating."

"Can you tell me one?"

"The worst one I heard was that she died."

He took a step backwards. "I...I don't–."

"Remember...that's just a story though, young man. Could be a lie." He pointed at him with the cigarette. "Was she an old girlfriend or something?"

"Nah...I just...I don't know...I read her book and..." it all sounded so dumb coming out of his mouth that he decided to stop while he was ahead. "Thanks for your time."

He got in his car and pulled off.

204

Tye sat outside in front of his house that he shared with Joanne for five minutes before finally going in. The only reason he was there was that he needed more clothing and he wanted to be sure he was moving in the right direction about not marrying her.

The moment he turned the knob, and entered the foyer, he could hear some soft moaning in the back of the apartment. Slowly he crept toward his bedroom door and opened it gently.

There as clear as day, he saw Joanne lying on her back.

Her eyes were closed.

Her legs were wide open as Logan was eating her pussy.

Apparently well.

Tye's jaw dropped. He didn't know what he expected to see, but he definitely didn't expect that. He also didn't care.

So he stood there and allowed her to reach her orgasm. He didn't want there to be any denial. He even snapped a picture on his phone for his records. When she was done he said, "Y'all good in there?"

"Oh my God!" She said, kicking him off of her with a foot to the forehead before snatching the sheets to cover her body.

Logan, being buck naked and in the open, sat on the edge of the bed, legs pressed tightly together. He dragged his hands down his face in guilt.

"Logan, I'm so sorry," she said to Tye.

"My name's Tye." He laughed. "That's Logan over there."

Wow. She fumbled majorly. "I mean T–."

"This makes sooo much sense." Tye said, shaking his head.

"Listen, it's not what you think. I–."

"Let me stop you, Joanne. Because this is exactly what it looks like. You in the apartment we shared, getting your pussy ate by my best friend because you thought I was still in the hospital. No need in lying. I saw it."

Slowly Logan looked at him. "Don't act like you're innocent, man."

Tye laughed. "So this is the part where you tell my girl about all the bitches I fucked behind her back right?"

"Nah, he already did that."

"Good...saves me time. Because let me make clear what I said to you in the hospital, bitch," Tye said. "We over, slut!"

"Tye, can we talk!" Logan yelled.

Tye grinned. "The irony is, she was the one thing I would have given you, if you would've just asked." He walked out.

Tye drove down the street with a smile on his face.

He never thought that seeing his best friend fuck his girl would put him in such a good mood.

But it did.

No longer did he have to fake like he wanted to be with her. No longer did he have to deal with Clark and the rest of the Davenports. He was free to...

Free too...

He slowed down and pulled over.

Free to do what?

He still owed a madman $150,000 at last count.

So sure, he had the illusion of freedom, but what was he going to do with it? How was he going to live? What was to happen with his business? He may have wanted to be done with Joanne but he couldn't see working alongside Logan anymore.

The other fucked up part was for the earlier years of his life his head was in the clouds. And so outside of his mother, sister, and father, he lost most genuine connections. And he didn't have anywhere to turn to at the moment.

He decided to go back to the old apartment.

And read the diary to catch up with a new friend.

When Tye opened his apartment door, he was angry to see Logan leaning against the wall dressed in the grey sweatsuit with the words The Lit they both owned. He had the hoodie over his head in shame.

"Hey, man," Logan said under his breath.

He would have to change the locks for sure.

He stood up straight. "Can we talk?"

Tye chuckled and moved to the kitchen. "Wow."

"Can you make me a drink too?"

He grabbed a water bottle. "Nigga suck my dick." He twisted the cap and took a big gulp. "And how the fuck did you get in here?"

"You gave me a key. Remember? Kept getting locked out." He sighed. "Listen, we need to talk about the restaurant."

"You want it?" Tye said plainly.

He frowned. "Wait, you serious?"

"Do you want it or not?"

"I mean...I could probably handle it on my own but..."

"It's like this, you came here for some reason so you must have a plan. If you don't have a plan you can get up out my crib, think of one, and come back."

"I came over here to explain to you that–."

"The trouble is you want me to be angry." Tye laughed. "And I'm not mad. I'm genuinely relieved."

"You want me to believe that–."

"Nigga, I don't care what you believe. I dodged a bullet with that bitch."

He nodded while looking into his eyes. "I believe you."

Tye shrugged and sat on the blow-up bed which was already deflating. "So now, if it's not about business, I don't know what you want from me."

"So, you don't care if we together?"

Tye spit out water. "You want to be with her?"

"Yes."

"How long?"

"How long what?"

"You bold as fuck, Logan. So you had to have been wanting her for a minute. Not surprised. Just asking for that time frame."

"From the moment I met her. At that festival. You probably don't recall but I spotted her first."

"I actually do remember."

"And even though I was standing next to you, she was interested in you instead of me. Don't get me wrong I didn't plot but..."

"I know you want this situation to be more romantic than it is with that tale. Nigga falls for a bitch; the bitch wanted his friend and now she wants the nigga. But I need to be clear. Had it been under any other circumstance you would be dead. Regardless of how many bitches I fucked or let suck my dick, you slept with my fiancé. Then you broke the cardinal rule by telling her about my past hits."

"I know."

"And to make shit worse you have yet to say my bad."

"I didn't think you were a man that wanted apologies."

"I'm a man who deserves respect. There's a difference. Say what you want about my character when it came to our bond, I never slipped or folded."

"I am sorry."

"I'll take that for what it's worth. Which is nothing. Now let me tell you what's about to happen. You gonna go to the Davenports and let them know that you were always in love with her or some shit like that. To be honest I don't care what you tell them niggas. What I do know is that you have to do a good job of convincing them that you gonna do right by her. And you gonna tell Clark you always felt this way. Make it romantic. Like you tried to do with me just now."

He nodded. "And then what."

"You can have the restaurant. I don't want it. Just give me fifty thousand and we done."

"But you always loved cooking."

"I still do. But the way I feel right now I gotta fall back. Not to get too sentimental but I got a lot of shit to work out. And running a business with a nigga who fucked my girl ain't in the cards for me."

Logan nodded. "Fifty K huh?"

"That's the plan."

Logan took a deep breath. "Thank you. I'll get the money to you in a couple days."

"I hope you feel that way when you get what you want. You know, officially into the family and shit with Joanne."

Tye laughed him all the way out the door.

A few days later, when Tye walked into the alley of his restaurant to get his money from Logan, he saw pandemonium.

There were police cars, several ambulances and even a fire truck parked in various forms in front of his business. As he made his way as close as he could get, he saw a murder scene.

There was shattered glass in front and inside the spot. There was blood splattered everywhere. But on one of the tables, lying face up was Logan with a gunshot wound to the chest. He was wearing a The Lit grey sweatsuit.

"What the fuck?" His heart dropped as he watched the paramedics tend to his lifeless body. "What the fuck happened," he whispered to himself.

"Somebody shot his ass." Run said, standing next to him. "Maybe they got him mixed up with another nigga. Maybe they didn't expect two niggas to dress alike?" He shrugged. "I don't know. What you think though?"

It wasn't until that moment that he realized he was there. "Wh...why?"

"I want my money. If you got a policy on his head then it's time to collect and pay up."

"I don't."

Run laughed. "That's a shame. Most business partners do." He shrugged. "Welp, his life bought you a few more days. I'll be back in seven for more blood or money." He pointed in his face. "That's gonna be up to you."

CHAPTER NINETEEN
CANDY APPLE

Logan's mother's face was buried into Tye's chest as he sat on her sofa consoling her.

Literally, the woman was so overcome with grief by the loss of her son, that she had fallen on her knees and into Tye's chest as she clutched his clothing.

"Oh my God, Tye. I don't understand. He was such a sweet boy. He would have helped anybody who asked. You know that."

Tye chose to fake ignorance. Because although Logan was a good friend in the past he'd also recently caught him sleeping with his fiancé. So his rep was flat.

"Yeah, he was a good dude."

"Then why this happen?" She sobbed.

He knew exactly why it happened. But what was he going to do, tell her about the beef he had with Run? There was no way he would even allude to knowing what went down.

Besides, the last thing he needed was the police reaching out to him and wanting answers.

"Is there anything I can do for you?" He really wanted her off of him so he could get out the door.

"No." She sniffled. "Not right now. Just come and check on me. He was my only boy. Do you hear me? My only boy. So I'm gonna need to lean on you now more than ever."

Tye's mind was still swirling.

He couldn't believe that Logan was murdered in their new restaurant. So as he drove down the street he thought about how he was going to come up with money that he didn't have access to directly.

One thing he was certain of is that Run was not playing games. He wanted his paper and he wanted it now.

When he looked down at his ringing phone he saw it was Joanne. He hadn't spoken to her since he saw her getting her box ate by the homie. He had to be strategic. The last thing he wanted her to keep in mind was that she was the reason that the wedding was off, not him. He figured if he gave

215

in and spoke to her at least once, then she could play the victim.

And he didn't want her having any control over him anymore.

Suddenly she stopped calling and sent a text message:

There is a party at your restaurant tonight. They say it's on you.

Oh shit. The birthday party.

Since everything is going on, I'll help your employees set things up. Please call me. I'm sorry about what I did. But I still believe we can make this work.

No the fuck we can't either. He said to himself.

So he ignored her.

Instead, he made a right turn off of Liberty Road when suddenly he saw her.

No, not Joanne.

The female who left the diary in his car.

Candy Apple.

His pressure rose.

He wanted to get at her so badly, he almost hit another car trying to make a U-turn back in the direction she went into. He saw her carrying several grocery bags in each hand and hoped they were heavy enough to prevent her from entering her apartment before he could speak with her.

Finally in front of her spot, he found a handicap parking space and left his car there illegally. Quickly he ran up the stairs leading into the building he saw her enter. His wishes went in his honor because the moment she walked into her apartment he pushed in behind her.

"What are you doing in my fucking..." She recognized him.

"You can't be in my–."

"The diary. I want to know who it belongs to."

She backed up and fell down in the recliner behind her. The bags of groceries spilled out onto the living room floor. "What are you–."

He rushed up to her and lowered his height. "Do you know the girl? Because I want to meet her!"

"Please, I don't want to get involved."

He frowned. "Don't want to get involved?"

"Yes...leave me out of it."

"So...so someone told you to give it to me? Was it my fiancé?"

Silence.

"Listen, I don't care about anything else." He rubbed her arms. "And I'm not mad. I just wanna know who the diary belongs to."

"Why should you be mad? You were the one who left me stranded in the alley and–."

"Is that what you really want to go with?"

She swallowed again. "What you talking about?"

"I waited for you to return for over twenty minutes. You didn't come back. So I know something else was up. I was supposed to find that book wasn't I?"

"I'm confused."

"Who does the diary belong to?!" He yelled. "Tell me her name. Now!"

She trembled. "I...I.."

In his mind she alone had the information he needed to find the woman. And he wanted to meet her. "I need her name."

"I don't know her name! I was paid to give it to you!"

Slowly he rose up. "Paid?"

"Yes."

218

"By who?"

"A girl."

"The girl in the diary?"

"I don't know. But I don't think so."

"Could you...could you see her collarbone or chest?"

"Yeah, we were at your party and she stepped up to me."

His words were careful. "Listen...did she have a strawberry tattoo?"

"No."

"Fuck!" He dragged a hand down his face. "Okay...what happened?"

"Like I was saying, this girl was at your party. She was looking around like she was hunting. About ten minutes later, she approached me. Since like I told you, you are a legend in the–."

"Fuck all that. Get back to the point."

"She said you needed to read the diary. She gave me some money. But didn't tell me much else. Although she was with some other lady too. I'm sorry. I really am. Did something happen?"

He dragged a hand down his face. "I need more!"

"That's all I know! Shit!"

He shook his head and stormed out.

CHAPTER TWENTY
TRASH

Joanne walked into the bustling restaurant in a hurry. There was a large plexiglass covering the window due to the bullets which had taken one of the owner's lives.

Large shades covered her eyes and her red hair was pulled up in a ponytail as if she were deeply grieving. Even though she and Logan just found each other, she was disappointed in his murder. Because unlike Tye, he appeared ready to risk it all to be in the family.

But he was dead.

So she had plans to redefine her relationship later with Tye.

As she moved deeper inside, several employees approached her claiming that Tye's sister was suspiciously hanging behind the register. And that's exactly where she found her when she walked in.

"Ava, what are you doing at the register?" She tossed her Fendi bag on the counter and removed her shades, placing them down.

A customer took a Sprite she handed him and walked toward the table.

"I just rung up a customer. What does it look like."

"But nobody said you could work here."

"This is my brother's restaurant. And I heard about Logan so I didn't want him working here alone."

"Tye got a whole staff! The nigga is never here. I mean, did he say you could do this?"

"This is my brother's–."

"Listen, I know whose restaurant this is. And again no one said you could work here. And even if you wanted to lend a hand, why you hanging behind the register instead of helping in the kitchen or some shit like that?"

"You don't even realize what's about to go down." She crossed her arms over her chest.

"What are you talking about?"

"You don't think that Logan died in here for nothing do you? Are you and the rest of the Davenports that stupid?"

"Be careful with me."

"I'm not afraid of you, Joanne. Nobody's afraid of you anymore. You washed up anyways. All I'm saying is there is a lot that is about to go down and if I were you I would take some time to get out of town before things come back on you. Like they did Logan."

"You threatening me and my father?"

"Nope. Just you."

She took a deep breath. She had no idea what Ava was talking about but she didn't care either. She wasn't interested in the restaurant business. She had no passion for owning her own place. But she realized she had to step up if nothing else to prove to Tye that she could be there when he needed her.

"Just get out."

Ava moved to walk around her. But Joanne grabbed her arm along with the purse on her shoulder first. Dipping inside, she fisted out handfuls of cash. "Bounce."

"Stupid bitch! I need that money."

"Girl bye!"

"I hope she ruins you too!" Ava said before taking off running.

"Who?"

She kept running.

"Who?!"

She pushed out the door.

223

The moment she left Joanne walked into the kitchen where the employees were still hard at work. She grabbed her phone from her purse and called the one man she could always count on.

"Daddy." She cried.

"What is it, baby girl?"

"I messed up."

"How?"

"I'm afraid to tell you. Because I don't want you to look at me differently."

"I could never do that."

"Do you promise?"

"Trust me, whatever is going on I can help you work it out. Now talk."

Tye felt like the world knew something he didn't.

When he first read that diary he assumed that he could immerse himself into someone else's world for the sole purpose of entertainment.

Voyeurism if you will.

But now it was becoming obvious that he was a part of it all. But how could that be possible? He knew none of the people in the diary.

He didn't know a Peter.

He didn't know a Penny.

And he didn't know a Nicole or Lala.

He was 100% sure that either the book was totally fiction or that the diary belonged to someone else trying to fuck up his mind. And yet if that was true what did the girl mean by saying someone paid her to give it to him?

The moment he pulled up at his apartment building and walked up the stairs he saw the man with the hoodie was actually a girl. She was sitting on the step.

Was she the one who paid the Candy Apple to give him the diary?

"Who are you?"

She rose. "I'm a friend of Run's." Her voice was deep. Masculine.

He forgot about him that quickly. "Okay what does he want?"

"At this point he's made himself clear. He wants his money."

"He just killed my best friend and–"

She immediately started laughing. "Like you give a fuck."

"What did you just say?"

"We know you don't care about him. We saw him with your fiancé. We also saw you walk into the apartment when they were having sex. We know you caught them. We also have video and voice recordings of them arguing when you were gone."

Tye's blood felt as if it ran cold. "You bugged my apartment?"

"Yep. The bookcase."

She smiled.

He knew something was off and he hated himself for not trusting his instincts. "So...so...y'all setting me up for murder?"

She giggled. It was a light chuckle that lit up the room and turned more feminine. "What does it mean to set someone up?"

"Stop playing with me!" Tye yelled. He was so angry that the girl, who was obviously strapped because her hand hovered over her hip, jumped.

"Did we make you ignore your fiancé?"

Silence.

"Did we force you to argue with your best friend over business?" She laughed. "Nah, you did that yourself. We just got the tapes."

He knew it was a far stretch but he decided to ask anyway. "Do you know anything about the diary?"

Before she answered he could tell by her expression that she was clueless. "You need to get Run's money. And you need to get it now."

"What happens if I don't?"

"Do you really want to ask that?"

"Since y'all seem to have the upper hand you might as well tell me. What happens if I don't get this money?"

"Well, we know you don't care about the girl. That much is obvious."

"I care about her. Just don't want to be with her."

"If that's what you call it. But we see it differently. I wonder how you would feel if something happened to your sister though. Or mother?"

Tye glared.

"Yeah, that would shake you. Right?"

The moment Tye entered his mother's apartment he was disgusted.

His mother had trash all over the floor. Nothing was clean. And he could smell the foul odor of food not being disposed of properly in the air.

Kicking past the trash he walked towards the back where his mother slept. The door was open and per usual the room was neat. He sat on the edge of the bed.

She was knocked out.

"Ma."

She didn't move.

"Ma, wake up." He nudged her hard.

She moved a little and smiled when she saw him. She smelled of alcohol and he knew immediately she was drunk.

"What you doing here?"

"Why does the house look like this, ma?"

"What you mean? My room is neat." She boasted.

"I'm serious. What about the rest of the place?"

"I haven't had time to clean it up. Been chasing behind your sister. She hasn't been home in four days. I mean, should I call child protective services? Because if I do that you know they'll blame me. They always blame me."

"I need you to get your life together." He said it as if it were simple when it was anything but.

"I thought you didn't want to have anything to do with me."

"You know I was mad."

"Tye, as many things that are going on in my mind right now, I can't be responsible for what you really mean. What I'm saying to you is that based on our last conversation I thought you didn't want to have anything else to do with me."

"I'm in trouble."

She glared. "But you been doing good. I know when you were younger there were issues but you came out of it and–."

"Being arrested and having a felony on my record is not something to be proud of."

"Why do you do that? Yes, your life was fucked up in the beginning but you turned it around. You invested in yourself. You got out of prison and came up with the plan. Give yourself some credit."

"You know there is nothing to be happy about with my life."

"If you're upset about that decision that you made for your father, when you were younger, then maybe it's time to make it right."

"I don't want to talk about that."

"You never do. Which is why you're having so much pain."

"Listen, I'm going to need you to go live with auntie for a little while. And I'll need you to chill there and not show yourself until things blow over."

"Is this about Logan?"

"Kind of."

Her brows rose. "You know what happened to him?"

He could see the fear in her face and realized telling her what he knew would be too heavy. Plus he didn't want to put her in a situation where she would have to testify against him. "No."

"Then what are you saying? Because you know before I live with my sister I would have to make sure it's worth it. We fight like cats and the people who hate them. It just wouldn't work. Not in the long term anyway."

"I don't need long term."

230

She sat all the way up. "Tye, you're scaring me. And you know I don't like fear."

"No one does. But I'm telling you, you should be scared, ma."

She sighed deeply. "This...this is..."

"Please, ma."

"But what about Ava? I don't want her coming back here if our lives are in danger."

"I'll find her."

"Are you sure?" She said with tears rolling down her cheeks.

They may have had a toxic relationship but in her own traumatic and tragic way she loved her daughter. "Listen, I will find her. Just get out of this house and lay low. I can't do what I have to do while worrying about you also."

"Okay. I don't know what this is about but you'll probably need to talk to your father too."

He took a deep breath. "I know."

CHAPTER TWENTY-ONE
WATER

Tye sat outside of his restaurant which he could see was being closed by the staff for the night. Although most customers would've been gone by now, the birthday girl appeared happy as she was carrying a bottle of Hennessy which was mostly empty in her arm on her way out the door.

Tye smiled.

He didn't have any hand in her happiness, but at least her event in his restaurant was a success. Because it would be the last event ever. As the staff and her friends ushered her out and toward the car, the lights in his business turned off.

When it was pitch black three of his cooks followed by Joanne walked outside. They looked exhausted. When everyone was out, his ex-fiancé locked the door, got in her car, and pulled off.

With the coast being clear, Tye exited his Benz and snuck into the restaurant. Slowly he entered and walked toward the back. First he grabbed many towels and tucked them under the doors. Next he grabbed a hose and turned the water on. He allowed the liquid to run over everything electrical first. Hot flashes sparked before he moved to the furniture and doused anything that was high-priced.

Then he dropped the sink hose to the floor.

When he was done, propped on top of a table and watched the flood build toward the far back. He hadn't expected the water to continue to fill up the way that it had but before long he realized that had he been standing on the floor it would reach his knees.

Flood doors, which he owned, prevented flooding from the outside. Unfortunately, this meant they kept the water inside his establishment too.

He waited five hours as water continued to douse everything in sight. He could hear other appliances short circuiting and realized if he wasn't careful he could start a fire, which ironically he didn't want to do.

In his mind fraud investigators always expected a fire. But few thought about the damage water could cause.

When he was sure he was done, and had fucked enough shit up, he jumped off the table. Water came to his waist until he opened the door and allowed it to roll outside and into the street.

Walking to his car, soaking wet, he pulled off and thought about hitting it to a motel room. He started to go back to his empty apartment, but he didn't feel like fussing with the air mattress or the stranger who obviously knew where he lived.

He wanted to be alone.

So he decided to do just that.

Tye went to the department store earlier to purchase grey sweats and a pack of white t-shirts. When he was done he checked into a motel, took a shower, and settled down. He didn't grab the diary. Or turn on the TV.

Instead he looked at the cell phone which sat next to him.

Waiting.

Two hours later Joanne called.

He didn't answer.

She called again.

He ignored her.

Finally she sent a text.

Something happened at Lit. Everything is destroyed. I think the staff members left water on. Please come home.

It was the message he was waiting on.

Now he could do what he wanted.

Reaching to his left, he grabbed the diary and sat it on the bed. For some reason he was suddenly fearful of its words.

Of its pages.

He didn't understand who wanted him to read the story.

Why was he targeted?

There was only one way to find out. He had to complete the book. Every last word. But instead of getting right down to business, the first thing he did was call his mother to be sure she was safe. "You good?"

She sighed. "Yeah. I'm still at your aunt's."

"You didn't let anybody follow you did you?"

She sighed again. "Tye, this is all so crazy. Why would anybody be following–."

"Did you check or not, ma?"

"Yes. I think we're good. Have you found Ava?"

"No. But I got a message from Joanne that she came to the restaurant and tried to steal money."

235

"Stealing money? From who?"

"The register."

"Ava, why..." she said to herself, calling her daughter's name.

"I don't know, ma. But I'm not worried. I went to her folks place earlier and she wasn't there. Hopefully she'll show up soon."

"Is everything okay? With you and Joanne?"

"Nah."

"Are you okay with everything not being okay?"

He smiled. "Never better."

"Are you sure it's over?"

He positioned himself so that his feet rested flat on the floor. "Yeah, ma. Why?"

"Because I never liked her."

He nodded. "Most people don't."

"I'm serious. She and her family were always snobby. I used to go to school with Clark. They had so much money but still went to public school. Couldn't afford the privates I guess. Yeah...couldn't stand them. They nothing like us."

"They say opposites attract." He was just talking at this point.

"True. But they didn't say always. Are you leaving her?"

"Yep."

236

"Well make sure you pack up your books. You been collecting them things since you were a kid. Don't want her selling them or nothing like that."

"She wouldn't do that."

"You don't know what a woman scorned would do."

He nodded again. "I'll be back in contact soon. Stay out the way though. Everything will blow over shortly."

"You seem awfully confident."

"I am. I have a plan. Praying it works."

"You don't know how good it makes me feel to hear that."

He smiled. "Aight, ma. Later."

When he hung up he laid across the bed with his hand on his tatted chest. Slowly his head turned toward the right.

Taking a deep breath, he picked up the diary and began to read its words.

****

May 14, 2008, 5:19 PM

Dear Diary,

It's been a long day.

Probably the longest I've ever had in my life.

Last week I buried my aunt. Cried so much I gave myself hiccups. I didn't know how that was possible. I checked it out yesterday though because the hiccups were so strong they felt violent.

Every time one hit me; I thought my throat would fall out.

I learned that prolonged crying irritates the diaphragm which causes an issue with the larynx.

I have never hiccupped that hard before. Embarrassment when everyone looked at me, as one blasted from my mouth, was the only thing that made me calm down.

Until...

Well...

After the funeral people were supposed to show up at the apartment I still lived in with Nicole. I was supposed to be moving out officially, but after auntie died, so suddenly, I didn't want to be there alone.

So, for reasons I blame myself for to the day, I didn't go.

I stayed in an apartment I hated.

Stayed around a cousin who hated me.

Stupid.

When I made it back to the apartment with Nicole, Penny, and Lala, we put out a cheese platter, some chips, and light snacks. People were supposed to be coming over later that day.

My aunt didn't have children but everyone knew how she felt about me. They knew how I felt about her. So why should we have to clean up behind people who claimed they wanted to be there for me in my time of need?

Once the food was set out and we waited for people to come, Nicole gave me "the look". It was when she lowered her brow and stared at me for a minute straight. Whenever she did this I would look away because I felt like she was going through a mental rolodex of all the things she hated about me.

"I thought you were supposed to be moving."

"I am."

"Leave her alone," Penny said.

She glared at her. "So you taking up for the girl who fucked your man?"

"You are a mean person. And one day you'll get what you deserve."

"That's wrong, Penny," Lala said.

"But it's true." I spoke.

Nicole took her eyes off of Penny and put them back on me. She wanted a punching bag. Not a boxer like Penny would have been.

"You a stupid bitch. I be glad when you're gone."

"And you're a thief." I spoke. "Did you tell Penny how you stole her money?" I paused. "Did you tell her how you were going to blame someone else instead? Probably me if I'd been around."

Nicole looked like she'd been dropped off a rollercoaster and I loved it.

"What money?"

"The money you said was missing from your bank account. You thought you were hacked. I was gonna tell you but the bank gave it back. But it was Nicole who did it."

"I didn't steal no money!"

"Yes, she did!" I yelled.

She wasn't getting out of that shit. Court was in session! I don't know where I got the strength, but I loved how it felt coursing through my veins.

"Did you take my money, Nicole?" Penny was trembling.

Nicole looked down and slowly back at Penny. "I was gonna put it back."

"And here you are, talking about her like you ain't the real snake around here."

That's when things got hazy. I don't know how she was able to get me. But Nicole moved quickly. Like a rattlesnake. She hit me first with fists. And for some reason, instinct I guess, I grabbed the soda bottle on my left and plopped her on the head.

It was glass.

Blood squirted from the side of her eye like a water fountain. And before long, she ran out screaming that I cut her.

I could hear her yelling from the streets.

"No matter what happens, I'll bail you out," Penny said as Nicole continued to yell from outside. "But you need to know she's gonna tell the police. And you are going to get locked up. And I'm so sorry." She hugged me for a minute and I held her back.

She was right.

I was locked up.

And I just got out.

CHAPTER TWENTY-TWO
LIQUID

Tye was in line at McDonald's with his face glued between the pages of the diary. His phone had buzzed so many times due to Joanne crying about the restaurant being destroyed, that he kicked it to silent.

The only calls he took were from his mother. And of course his sister who he had yet to find.

Flipping the pages he got back into the book.

****

May 24, 2008, 4:30 PM

Dear Diary,

My aunt left me $150,000 from her insurance policy.

And that's when things changed with me and my boyfriend. I spent a lot of money on him, but I knew I had to leave the apartment I shared with Nicole, which I did, so we got a place together.

He asked me for money from time to time.

I gave it to him usually.

But I wanted to save some.

So I was careful to not live beyond my means.

I quit my job so this was all the money I had left. Which as of that moment was $140,000.

Things changed with us.

But I don't think it was because of the money.

Whenever we had sex in the past, it always felt like he needed me for a release. And I didn't mind because I needed him too.

Lately though, it felt like he wanted to have sex for a reason. A reason that I didn't quite understand. I don't know if it's possible to love a person as much as I do with Peter. But if it is, if someone else out there understands me, it'll make what happened over the next year make sense.

It'll make things not seem so crazy.

He tended to want sex with me from the back. When I asked why, he said from the back, was the closest to a woman's G-Spot. He says he could only get pleasure from me if he knew I was being pleased.

It didn't feel bad.

Just different.

He said he knew a lot about women.

We were both young so how can somebody so young know so much?

Sometimes I feel like I ask too many questions. Am I asking so many questions that I forget to have fun? To enjoy life? To make the best of the situation while I'm in it?

No, I think it's that I always feel like someone is plotting against me.

So as he was making love to me, from the back, I felt his body tremble.

More like a volcano about to explode.

As I write these words I feel crazy. And yet this is exactly what it felt like. Like he was on the verge of a heightened experience.

Normally he would pull out. Unless we were using condoms. But as the sensation took over him I felt him pushing deeper into my body.

"Pull out, Peter." I said softly.

"W...what baby?"

"I said pull out. I feel you shaking."

"I'm not gonna cum inside you."

"But it feels like you already have."

"So you don't want to have sex with your man?"

244

Just the thought of not pleasing him made my stomach queasy. Part of the reason I allowed him to do so many things to me when we had sex was because I wanted to please him.

"Of course I want to have sex with you."

"Then..... then...trust me."

"But...but what if I get pregnant."

"Then have my baby."

This scared me.

"I don't want to because–."

"You know what." He angrily pretended to pull out of me and cum on my back.

I know he pretended because when he placed himself on my skin I didn't feel that warm stream of liquid that I had before.

There was no need for me to ask him if he did what I already knew he didn't.

I wasn't going to quit him for lying either.

So I chose to leave it alone.

My life will never be the same.

CHAPTER TWENTY-THREE
WEIGHTS OF THE WORLD

The investigators contacted Tye about his restaurant and met him in the motel he was staying in for the past week. They had a lot of questions. Some theories and even more suspicions.

They wanted to know if he had more information on the flood. They wanted to know if he was there the night things happened. He answered flatly, lying of course, and coolly brushed the accusations they threw his way off.

The only thing he said was that whoever killed his best friend, must have destroyed his property too.

"That property has been there for over sixty years." One investigator said. "And now all of a sudden this happened?"

"Yeah." He said, raising his hands in the air. "I'm shocked too, sir."

"If that's true, what have you done in life to warrant so much hate?" He pointed at him with a pen.

For some reason, he thought about the question seriously. The truth was he had done many things. But he was personally responsible for this shit. "I don't know."

The investigator sighed. "That's all for now."

The moment they left; he picked up the diary for more answers.

****

June 24, 2009, 3:00AM
Dear Diary,

I haven't written you in a while.

A lot has happened.

I had a baby.

I think he did it on purpose. Which is why he kept having sex with me from the back.

But why?

I didn't realize how sick I would be while I was pregnant. How much it would take out of me. And every time I tried to think about what to write inside of you, I realized nothing meaningful would come out.

For some reason I wanted to pour all of my attention and love into the moment. I wanted to be fully present for my baby.

My little boy.

So I avoided you.

He's beautiful too. So perfect.

I know mothers say that all the time. That their babies are this or that, but my baby really is the best. He hardly cries. He laughs at everything. It's almost like he has no fear. Maybe I did a good job of making it clear that I will always be there.

That I would never abandon my baby.

But Diary, I fear Peter doesn't want our son.

He says babies are weights of the world.

It made me wonder, what happened so dark in his life to make him feel this way.

Tye closed the diary.

He sat up straight in the bed. Something was starting to feel...off.

Way off.

Different.

And yet realer than it had before.

He wanted a drink but had sworn it off for the moment. He wasn't refusing to drink due to a moral issue. He just needed to think clearly. He wanted to make sure he didn't miss a thing.

An attack against him.

248

An attack against his family.

And an attack, quite possibly, from the words of the book.

Slowly he picked it up and continued.

He says babies are weights of the world.

It made me wonder, what happened so dark in his life to make him feel this way.

I couldn't conceive what he meant. How could babies weigh down the world? Even as I write to you again, I can't imagine anything even close to babies not being anything other than love.

I needed a friend.

Motherhood can be lonely.

So my cousin Penny came back to visit me from Texas. She helped me get around the house. She sat with my baby boy so I could get some sleep. She did all she could to be an amazing friend.

And she was.

After some time, she was so kind, that my mind played tricks on me. And I started thinking it was for a different reason. Was she sleeping with Peter? Were they spending time in each other's arms at night?

For revenge?

"Can I ask you something?" I spoke.

"Of course."

I looked at my baby sleeping in the bassinet and back at her. "Why do you...why do you help me like this?"

She giggled. "What do you mean?"

"I'm serious."

"Because we family."

"But what about the history?" Greg's name floated in my mind although I didn't say the word.

"You mean with you and that dog of a man?"

"Yes."

"Because I know it wasn't your fault. I know now how manipulative Nicole is. And...and I know you still hold onto guilt. And I want you to know I forgive you, so you can let it go."

"I don't feel guilty anymore."

"You do."

She was right.

"I gotta be honest," she said.

"I'm listening."

"Nicole is mad."

I remember frowning. "About what? I don't even talk to her anymore."

"She's jealous. And that's the worst kind of evil."

"About...about what?"

"That you were left all that money. For some reason, I think she feels that had she known you were going to get it, that she would have kept you around to access it too." She shook her head. "She is...dangerous."

I should've listened.

****

June 27, 2009, 1:30 AM
Dear Diary,

I was sound asleep until I realized I hadn't written to you for a couple of days. But the reason I'm up is simple.

I'm scared of Peter.

The thing is, he's never been directly mean to me. I've always been a willing participant in his madness. Really, it's true. He's never yelled at me longer than a few seconds. And we don't fight or argue most times.

I allow him to control me.

He allows me to be with my baby.

I can't say we are boyfriend and girlfriend in the way we started out. But I do know one thing.

I'm a mother first.

And so, I decided to buy a home for me and my baby.

A place we can live and be happy together.

And Diary, I don't want him to come.

I don't want him around.

I just don't know how to tell him.

****

July 1, 2009, 2:30 PM

Dear Diary,

I woke up to find Peter holding our baby.

He never holds our son.

He told me one time that he was afraid of babies. Afraid he would hurt them.

So why is he holding the baby now?

"We have to talk." He spoke.

I jumped up, removed the baby from his arms and said, "Okay."

"I think we need to spend more time together."

"Okay." He's safe now.

"You don't have anybody else to get the baby?"

"Get the baby for what?"

"I said what I said." He sat next to me. "I want us to go out more. Spend time with each other." He looked at the baby and back at me. "Alone. I'd think you'd be happy."

"Peter, I am happy to spend more time with you, but I don't have any place to–."

"What about your cousin?"

"She's out of town."

"I mean the other one. Who you lived with."

"Nicole?"

"Yeah. I think that's her name. I mean she should be hard up for money now. Use her."

I hated him at that moment. Hate was something I wasn't always accustomed to. But if he thought I would hand my baby over to that monster, after everything she'd done to me it meant he didn't know me.

So who did he think I was?

CHAPTER TWENTY-FOUR
SHEEP

T ye, sat on the hood of his car talking to his mother at his aunt's house. Very rarely did he look up at the sun. But it was so beautiful that he found himself staring up at it from time to time. Taking in its glory, as if it would be the last time.

"Are you listening?"

Just like he thought, his mother had gotten into a fight with his aunt who said the words she'd heard many times before. "Get out her damn house."

"Tye, she said I have to leave. And I don't have any money to–."

"You can stay at my old apartment."

"It's empty."

"I renewed my lease. And I'll put a bed inside for you. Ava too if she wants to come."

"Where are you staying?"

"Been crashing at a motel. I'll be fine."

"Are you sure though?"

"Yes."

She leaned in and kissed him. She smelled of liquor so much that suddenly he wanted a drink. But he refused to indulge. "Look...I gotta go."

"Don't you always." She smiled at him, begging for something he couldn't provide. "I just...wish I could see you more."

"Not now."

"What's going on with you, Tye?"

He took a deep breath. Words wanted to leap from his lips but he was having trouble organizing them.

"Tye, honey, talk to me."

"I...I'm not sure but I think something is happening that I won't be able to get out of."

"Got to do with Logan again?"

"Yeah." He lied.

She nodded. "You can get out of this. I know you can."

He touched her face and kissed her cheek. Dipping into his pocket, he handed her the keys to his apartment and a few bucks. "Go to my crib. I'll see you when I can. And, ma, I do love you."

He got in his car and pulled off.

Tye tossed his keys on the bed and looked at the diary which sat on the end table.

It was becoming clearer that he was involved, although he hoped what he was reading would lead him to another direction.

Sitting on the edge of the bed, he opened the book and continued reading its words.

****

July 14, 2009, 3:13PM

Dear Diary,

He sat next to me on our couch.

Our knees touched and I could tell he wanted something from me I couldn't provide. It was in the way he gripped my hand.

His was sweaty.

Mine was heating up.

I didn't know what it was, but his touch felt different these days.

Colder.

More distant.

256

"My father got arrested."

He didn't really talk about his family. I didn't know much about them. Just that the relationship was bad and that he was looking for an escape. I think when we moved together when I got that money the escape was me.

"Again?"

"I need...I need your help to get him out."

"How much?"

"Fifty thousand."

I slid my wet hand away from his. "What about...the baby?"

"What about him?"

"I can't...I...I have to make sure we have money. I...I'm a mother now and I need to feel safe. I can't feel safe if I–."

"If I don't give him the money, my mother and baby sister will be out on the streets. So I need the funds."

"I...I'm sorry."

"Not even for me?"

"The baby is..."

He jumped up and stood over me. I remember thinking that he's finally going to hit me. That he was finally going to hurt me. I wanted him to do it too. Because that would be the excuse I needed to leave him now instead of later.

He didn't hurt me that day.

But he would hurt me soon enough.

****

July 15, 2009, 1:25PM
Dear Diary,

I found a house.

It was a small house. Nothing big or showy. If showy is even a word. But it was perfect for me and my son.

There was a backyard. As of now there were tiny ditches scattered throughout. Like someone dug it up just for fun. If you weren't careful you could break your leg. But I didn't care. I knew that once I fixed it up it would look like I wanted in my mind.

I would put a swing set in the back. A place where my baby could throw a ball. A wooden fence already separated that house from the others so I wouldn't have to do much but sit on my patio, drink lemonade, and watch him do life.

It had two bedrooms.

A tiny kitchen.

And a cute yellow bathroom with lavender flowers throughout.

The agent said with the money I was putting down on the house it would be mine.

Paid in full.

I never had a place I didn't have to share with other people.

Now I would.

Oh and Diary, I'm not taking Peter with me.

It's official now.

I just have to let him know.

****

July 16, 2009, 1:11AM

Dear Diary,

He came home just now.

Had been gone for hours.

But I noticed he had been bringing large black trash bags in the house every night. Sometimes he would go into the closet in the living room and spend hours opening and closing bags.

One time I saw white stuff on his black shirt.

I wondered what it was.

But I didn't dare ask.

But today, I had just put the baby down. And I was curious. Now that I think about it, it's like he always comes when the baby is asleep. But where does he go during the other times? I don't really care because...

I mean...

I prefer when he's not home. I don't think it's a secret because we don't speak much anymore. But I could tell he wanted to speak to me now.

"Hey...can we talk?"

I sat on the sofa. "Okay."

He sat at the kitchen table. I had to turn my head if I wanted to see him. I didn't do it right away though.

"I found that book with your pictures."

I could tell he was drunk. "What book?"

"The photo album. From when you were a little girl."

I nodded.

"I saw your mother too."

Now I turned my body to see his face. My hands gripped the back and my chin rested on the sofa. Now that I think about it I probably looked like a little girl. Peeking.

And hoping he'd say something nice.

"She was pretty. Your mother."

"Thank you."

"Why should you be thankful? You ain't have shit to do with it."

I nodded my head in agreement.

He was being mean again.

But he was also right.

"You know, when I found you throwing up on the side of that apartment building, the day I first met you, I did you a favor."

I continued to listen.

"I could tell what type of girl you were."

"What...what type of girl am I?"

"The kind that needs to be grateful. Grateful that a nigga like me would have anything to do with you. I hate bamma bitches. Always have. Always will."

I wanted to cry, but I convinced myself that he wanted me to cry too. And I wanted to be strong. Like Penny said I had to be.

"I am thankful you chose me."

"Then how come you don't act like it?" His teeth were clenched.

"Peter, what do you, what do you want? The money? Because I can give you a thousand but I found a house and–."

"Fuck that house! And fuck you too!"

My voice lowered. "Then...then what do you want from me?"

"I want you to recognize the kind of man I am, and the kind of woman you are too. You were never in my league."

"You're acting like Nicole."

He glared.

I don't know what made me say it. But I didn't want to take it back. I felt like, like I needed to defend myself like Penny said. Like maybe I was being pushed over too much and too often.

I'm tired of being the rock on the ground people kick out the way.

I want to be seen for who I am. A nice person. A black woman. And more than anything, a mommy.

"You a sheep." He continued. "And I'm a shepherd. Bitches like you will always need a nigga like me."

"That's not true."

He laughed and said words to me I'll never forget. Because it went so far against what I'd heard from him before.

And these words...dear Diary...changed me forever.

"You an ugly girl. Your eyes are too far apart. Based on the pictures, your weight ain't been steady since your mama died. And the only thing cute on you is the strawberry patch tattoo on your left shoulder."

Tye closed the diary.

He paced the floor next to the bed. Things were starting to come together like puzzle fragments in his mind. Still not clear but begging to be put back together for old times sake.

Before he could dive back in, his phone rang. He answered without knowing who was on the other line.

"Yes, can I speak to Tye Gates?"

"Who this?"

"This is your insurance company. For your restaurant."

"What about it?" He stared at the diary as he listened to her words. Mostly afraid.

"We're calling about the claim for your items."

He sat down. Had he been caught? "You mean my restaurant?"

"We discovered that there were some faulty pipes in your building and the adjoining units. The leasing company had major violations, due to the property being so old, by the state. They know it too. So they cut a check which covers all of your damages and your inconveniences. Can you come by tomorrow?"

CHAPTER TWENTY-FIVE
SUITCASES

Tye drove to his old neighborhood slowly.

The moment he crept down the street, he felt his stomach churn. He hadn't been in that neighborhood in over ten years. He didn't want anything to do with it to be honest.

But he was there today.

Pulling up into the driveway, he could see his father on his knees doing something but he couldn't see what. His motorcycle sat in the center of it all. A set of woman's legs dangled over his shoulder. From his position in the car he couldn't see her body or her face.

But he knew sex was involved.

So he waited until he heard her scream and when she was done, he walked over to them and stuffed his hands into his pockets.

"Oliver," the woman said, nudging his shoulder. "Oliver, someone's here!"

He wiped his mouth with the back of his hands and stood up.

She hopped off the boxes and said, "I'll wait for you in the house." She rushed past him, easing her panties out of her pussy in the process.

"Where is she?" Tye said.

He smiled. "Finally figured it out."

"Where is Ava?" He paused. "Because I know she's here. I knew she was here all along. Just didn't feel like coming by."

He grinned and wiped his mouth again. "She's with her friend."

Tye looked down. "I never...I never got a chance to..." He took a deep breath, dragged his hands down his face. "Why...why were you the way..."

"What?"

"Why were you the way you were? When we were kids?" He paused. "Why are you the same way now?"

"So you bring all of this on me now?"

"I'm asking. And I never asked you for nothing. I never asked you for shit. So I'm asking you why didn't you come home? Why did you treat ma the way you did? And why are you doing the same shit to Ava?"

"I never came home because the house was always nasty. She was nasty. And I didn't want to be around that shit."

266

"You were the reason the house was the way that it was! I remember you coming home, drunk, bringing your biker friends with you! Making a bunch of noise on school nights! I remember ma trying to clean up what looked like major parties going down every night. But she could never keep up with you and your disrespectful friends."

Oliver glared.

"And I remember when you would sober up, even if all of the filth and throw up from you and your friends was your fault, that you wouldn't stay the night if the bedroom was a mess. So she would keep the bedroom clean because it was the only place your friends wouldn't come. She was hoping that a clean room would be comforting for her husband. And I remember keeping my room together hoping you would be a father to me."

He glared.

"Is that what this is about? I mean, ain't you a little too old to be still wanting a daddy?"

"Nah...it's about the money...that you...that you had me trick..." Tye couldn't even say the words.

"What money?"

"The money that ruined my life. That I got for you."

He laughed. "Let's have a drink. Come inside so–"

"I don't want a fucking drink! I want you to acknowledge the shit that you did to me! When I was a kid. When I was–."

Oliver stepped back. "After all these years, you still weak."

"I'm not weak."

"Then you worrying about shit that don't matter no more. Either way it makes you less than a man."

Tye shook his head.

Oliver stepped closer. "Listen, the best thing I can do is tell you this. I don't remember the years that are important to you. I don't remember the house being messed up. Or the rooms being dirty or clean. I remember living my own life on my own terms. And the moment you realize that you will never get from me what you want...and that you will never make me feel guilty about the past, it will be the moment you can live your own life too."

"Oliver, hurry up!" The young girl said, peeping her head around the corner.

"Get the fuck back in the house!" He yelled. "Don't you see me talking to my son?"

"Okay..." she giggled before running back inside, feet slapping away.

"Look, I gotta go see about..."

"Yeah, I know." Tye shook his head, got in his car, and pulled off.

Joanne looked at Tye as he removed his clothing from the drawer and tossed them into one of the two suitcases on the bed in their room.

"So this is it huh?" She asked.

"Yeah."

She flopped down and looked at the wall. "Wow."

He sat next to her and looked ahead too. "You know...none of this shit is your fault."

She looked over at him. "What you mean? You caught me cheating. This has to be my fault."

"Before I met you I had a lot of shit going on. Stuff I never dealt with. And I...I..." He looked down. "I saw my pops carry shit certain ways with women and I..."

"Tye, what's up?"

"I think things are about to go bad for me. And to be honest I'm looking forward to getting it over with."

"You're confusing me now."

He chuckled. "I'm confusing myself." He looked over at her. "I know a lot has gone down between you and I over the last couple of days. Months for that matter. And I'm going to tell you honestly that your father will continue to cause problems for you if you let him."

"So this about my father now?"

He placed a hand over his heart. "I don't have any reason to lie to you, shawty. Not anymore."

"Well he's trying to cause problems for you too. Since you aren't going to marry me."

"I think he changed his mind. After the video I sent him earlier today."

"What video?"

"Of you and...Logan. Fucking."

"You recorded us? Why did you do that shit?"

"I need my family safe, and I can't be bothered with looking over my shoulder and my family's. I already got one nigga after me. I don't need two."

She didn't know what he meant with two but she said, "So he saw me...he saw me..."

"Yes." He paused. "And I know it's fucked up but he put me in that situation." He took a deep breath. "Joanne, you got to get a hold of him. Because no matter what your father does he's not going to convince me or anybody else to marry you. If you can believe it or not I got something bigger on my plate that I have to handle."

"Logan?"

"Even bigger than that."

"What's going on? Why don't you tell me? We could at least still be friends even if it's no longer a relationship. Or marriage."

"I'm not involving anybody else in my problems. I just want you to know that you will find somebody. But all this goofy shit that your father is doing with bullying niggas ain't it."

"I know you're right but I don't even know how to stop it."

"Have a conversation with him. Tell him how you truly feel. And be ready for the response because you may not like what he has to say. I had to do that recently. I went to my father expecting one thing and got another. But you know what, at least it was the truth. And I can handle the truth."

"The diary changed you somehow. Whatever is inside those pages made you different huh?"

It was getting too sentimental.

He got up and closed his suitcases. Holding one in each hand he kissed her on the cheek. "I'll come back later for my books."

"I know you will."

"You know, you still sexy. With or without the makeup."

She smiled. "You finally just figuring that out?"

Her head hung low as he walked out the door.

Tye waited at the park for Run.

When he parked his car he saw he was already there. Slowly he eased out and approached him.

"I'm not gonna lie, I didn't think you would come through with the money," Run said, rubbing his palms together. "Glad you applied yourself."

"He handed him a bookbag stacked with money. "I take it we done now."

Run took the bag and looked inside. "I don't know. I kind of gotten used to seeing you."

"Yes or no, man."

He flung the bag over his shoulder. "I wish I could give you an answer. But to be honest, it's not my answer to give."

"Then whose answer is it?"

Run smiled and moved toward his car.

"Whose answer is it?"

"You'll find out soon, Mr. Gates." Run said getting into the car. "You don't want karma coming back on you. Again."

Tye stood in the parking lot as he watched him drive away.

CHAPTER TWENTY-SIX

GAS LIGHT

****

July 24, 2009, 4:15PM

Dear Diary,

Something so bad happened and I have to write it all down before I forget.

Yesterday Peter came home in a hurry. He told me he needed me to do something and if I didn't do it soon, we could all be in trouble.

All of us?

"What is it?" I asked while watching him pace the floor.

"I have to be honest with you."

"Okay...what...what is it?"

"I'm a drug dealer."

I remember being still when he told me those words. I don't know what I thought Peter did, but selling drugs was not one of the things. How could I know? He was so secretive with everything in his life.

He didn't speak about his father.

He didn't speak about his mother.

And he didn't speak about his sister.

Tye closed the diary inside the motel room and looked out the window.

He was finally understanding what was going on. He was finally understanding what he was reading.

He was reading his own story, from his ex-girlfriend's point of view.

Plopping on the edge of the bed, he thought about how stupid he could have been not to see it before. And then he remembered a story in the newspaper years ago he read.

An old one too.

In it, a family consisted of four girls. Each recounted different versions of living in what was described as a real-life horror house. Some of them had traumatic experiences with their father while the oldest spoke about how amazing he was.

What was particularly striking was that despite the shared events, like birthdays and holidays, they all had different points of view. Different reactions and therefore different memories.

The word salience came up in the article.

Salience is the quality of being particularly noticeable or prominent.

For instance two passengers in a car who experienced an accident might recall different events from separate sides of the vehicle. The driver is probably more inclined to recall events occurring on the left and front of the car. While the passenger is more apt to remember things on the right which they noticed or found important.

Tye didn't remember because the personal account of his ex-girlfriend was not salient to him.

It was unimportant.

But to her it was everything.

And it would be everything to him now too.

****

He didn't speak about his father.

He didn't speak about his mother.

And he didn't speak about his sister.

"You sell drugs?"

"Yes, and now the police are coming. Because they been seeing you take the bags out the house."

"The bags you had me take to my car the other day?"

"Yes."

"But I didn't know what was in them! I didn't know what you were doing!"

"They didn't catch me. They saw you taking the bags to the car though. And they are on the way to lock you up now. Not me."

The room felt like it was spinning again.

"What can I do? What about the baby?"

"You have to go on the run right now, and I'll take care of everything."

"But...but where do I go?"

He reached in his pocket and handed me a hundred bucks. "Just go out for a couple of hours. And then call me. I'll tell you when to come back."

"Okay, let me pack the baby's bag. He's sleeping and–."

"No! If you take the baby they will put him in foster care if you're arrested." He shoved me toward the door. "Just go! I'll get everything cleared up. I promise."

"Please don't forget to feed him! He's–."

"Go! I got him. I promise. I won't let anything happen to him."

Scared about being arrested, I rushed out the door and took his car since they were looking for me in mine. I was so afraid of getting locked up for drugs I didn't know what to do.

I couldn't be arrested and leave my baby.

I couldn't trust him to take care of him forever.

So I did what he told me, hoping he'd clear it up.

I just drove.

I drove so far the gas light came on. And when I filled it up, I drove again.

A few hours later I called the house and Peter didn't answer. A couple hours after that he still didn't answer the phone.

And my heart dropped.

Where was he?

More importantly, where was my baby?

CHAPTER TWENTY-SEVEN
WOLF

Tye pulled up in front of the building of the girl who left the diary in his car.

After parking, he walked up the stairs and stood next to the apartment door. He heard her voice inside.

She was loud.

Boisterous.

And home.

The moment he knocked, he heard footsteps slide toward him and then silence. He took a deep breath.

"I'm not here to hurt you." He said from the hallway.

"Then what are you back here for?"

"I have a picture I need you to look at."

"I don't want to get involved in–."

"Please."

"Why should I?"

"My life been fucked up since I got this book. The least you can do is help me."

It seemed like forever, but finally the door unlocked and opened. However, the chain was secure. If he wanted to kick it in he could but this meeting wasn't about that. It was about something much deeper.

So he reached into his pocket and removed his cell phone. After a few taps he showed her the picture. "Is this the girl who paid you at that party?"

She looked at him and then looked down.

"Please. Just answer the question."

She nodded slowly. "Yes."

"What did she say to you?"

"She seemed frustrated. Like somebody made her do it. I remember thinking that even though the money was good and the job seemed easy, I felt like I would pay more in the future somehow. And since you showed up at my house asking questions, I guess I was right."

"I don't get it."

"It felt forced. Like she wasn't the one asking. But my rent was overdue and to be honest I was bored. And since I knew who you were I was also intrigued."

He was so annoyed he could scream. "Did she say anything about the person who gave her the book?"

"The book?"

He took a deep breath. "The diary."

She giggled. "You have a problem saying diary don't you? I remember when I was asked to leave it in your car. I thought to myself, what man would actually read this thing. And now I get it. A man who is ashamed of his love for literature."

"I'm not ashamed."

"Then maybe you're ashamed of your love for stories. Or lies."

His jaw twitched. "Did she say anything else?"

"No. Just to get you the *book* as you would say, the best way I could. So I fucked you and dropped the bitch off in your car." She shrugged.

"Wow."

"I would have done that for free." Suddenly the chain came off the door.

Uninterested, he shook his head and walked away.

Tye tried to use the key in the apartment he once shared with Joanne.

It didn't work.

He shook his head, smiled, and knocked two times.

"Who is it?"

"It's me." He spoke.

She scurried to the door and opened it wide. "Hey, stranger."

He nodded. "Changed the locks already?"

"I mean, you said you didn't want me anymore. And I don't know, before the locks were changed I kinda still felt like I was waiting on you to...to..."

"Come back?" He spoke.

She took a deep breath. "Are you coming back?"

Silence.

It was clear at that moment he wasn't. "So what are you here for?"

He pointed in the direction the books were posted. "My things."

She smiled, shook her head, and looked down. "You know what...I always felt like you loved those books more than me." She opened the door wider. "Now I know it's true. Come in."

He went to the closet and grabbed three unassembled boxes to pack everything inside. He assembled one as she looked on.

"So where you going?" She asked, sitting on the sofa. "Are you moving in with some cute girl?"

"Nope."

"So where you taking the books?"

"I'll take them to my old place."

"You kept it?"

"Logan didn't tell you that?"

She shook her head no.

"Guess y'all weren't as close as you thought."

"Touché'."

He grinned.

"So what were you looking for the other day? On the shelf."

"A camera."

"A camera? Did you find it?"

"Nope...it's gone."

"Who was filming us?"

"A long story."

She sighed. "So, are you gonna move back into your old place or just use it for storage?"

"Staying at a motel room until..."

"Until what?"

Silence.

"Until what, Tye?"

"Until it's my time to..." His sentence was cut short when one of the first books he had been given as a child fell from the shelf. It was an Aesop fable and he remembered being afraid of it when he first read the words as a little boy.

He picked it up.

"What's that?"

It wasn't until that moment that he realized he was still in her crib because he was having an out of body experience. Walking over to her he sat down with the thin tale in his hands. "The Boy Who Cried Wolf."

"Oh...that's the story of the boy who told lies about a wolf coming to his town and then he learned not to lie."

"Nah. That's the newer version. The ones for Americans. In the older version, this one right here, Peter was eaten along with the she...she...sheep."

"What's wrong?"

He shook his head and smiled.

The name Peter, that he read about in the diary over the last few weeks was based off of the story on his shelf. A reference he didn't catch because to be honest, he didn't care.

"What is it, Tye?"

"This story...always got me." He smiled and shook his head while feeling stupid. "Because I never understood why the boy's father gave him

284

such a harsh job. To be in charge of guarding sheep from the wolf. I always felt like his father..."

"Let him down?" She asked.

He rose. "I gotta go."

"What about your books?"

"I'll be back for them." He ran out the door.

Ava was just coming out of her father's house when she saw her brother leaning on his car.

She frowned. "What you doing here?"

"I know you paid the girl. At my party."

She slowly walked up to him, while looking down at her nails. "What girl?"

"I'm not mad at you, Ava."

Finally her head rose.

"Where is she? I mean, is she out of jail?" He asked.

Silence.

"Is she home or not, Ava?"

"A girl didn't pay me. A nigga with more tattoos on his face than you did." She shook her head. "I was scared. He threatened me. But I heard you did her wrong."

The true words hit him hard. "I...I know."

"Do you though?"

He looked away.

"How could somebody make up such a vicious lie? How could you...how could you do that to someone who cared about you?"

"I was young."

"You were evil."

He wanted to argue but as she spit word after word he had to ask himself, *where was the lie?*

"I know. But I have to know is she, is she out?"

"She will find you."

"So I take it that the answer is yes?"

Silence.

"How much did they pay you? To give me the book."

"Diary." She paused. "Does it even matter?"

He sighed. "I want you to know that I'm going to make this right."

She nodded. "I hear you."

He stood up straight. "But you got to make shit right too."

"I don't have nothing to do with–."

"Part of the reason I'm in this shit is because of dad." He paused. "And I know now that he could never have been to me what I wanted. A father. But you can make the best of shit right now by doing right by ma."

"I hate that bitch. She's toxic as fuck."

"She is." He looked at the house. "But that nigga in the house is worse. Because he doesn't give a fuck about you. He'll run up your credit, get you to do dangerous shit and not come to the rescue. Ma may be a drunk but she does care."

Her eyes widened. "What did dad do to you? Like what happened? With that girl and–."

"When the time is right I'll tell you. But I want you to give ma the same grace as you do that nigga. And when he tells you how he is, believe him." He paused. "I didn't and now I gotta pay for it. Possibly with my life."

He kissed her on the cheek, got in his car and drove off.

CHAPTER TWENTY-EIGHT
CONFUSION

Tye sat on the edge of the bed and looked out into the room.

All of his things remained in boxes because he knew he wouldn't be staying where he was for long. And it was time to come face to face with his biggest lie. One so huge it hurt people.

One of them, his own flesh and blood.

Grabbing the diary on the end table, he opened it up and read the words.

****

Present Day 2:34 AM

Dear Diary,

This is my last entry.

By now it may be clear that I wrote this book after the worst thing in life ever happened to me. My boyfriend and my vicious cousin plotted against me. I never felt a pain so lasting.

And since I lost my mother, aunt, and baby, you must believe that my words are true.

Every word of this was written in the most constrictive place imaginable. A prison cell. I wrote these words while hearing the cries of other inmates begging to go home.

The cries of inmates wanting their mother.

The cries of inmates wanting to be free.

At first I judged them.

Said to myself I'm not like them. I quickly learned I was wrong. I may not have stolen from anyone. I may not have hurt anyone intentionally. But I never stood up for myself in the way that I should have.

At the risk of avoiding confusion, I will maintain the name Peter.

But you know who you are.

Don't you?

When Peter told me to leave the house and leave my baby it took me two weeks to realize it was all a set up. It's amazing how vulnerable you can be entrusting someone due to misguided loyalty.

Prior to meeting Peter no one really saw me. And even though later I learned that he couldn't be trusted, my mind could not fathom anyone creating a lie so vicious.

But he did.

He had me believing that I committed some crime simply because I lived with a man who wanted something from me.

My money.

When I finally came back after traveling for three days and realized it was all a lie at my expense, several things happened.

First, I returned to the apartment only to discover he had moved.

Second, he had drained all of the money in my bank account. I didn't have one dime left.

The only reason I came back at all was because I wanted my baby. Because he had long since stopped accepting my calls. And he stopped sending me the few dollars needed to survive.

But fuck all of that!

Where was my child?

He was nowhere to be found.

I tried to go to the same places Peter went when I knew him briefly. But his mother told me he was no longer there. His father pretended to help me, by inviting me into his home. For my efforts it took me fifteen minutes to fight him off my body.

I was overcome with grief.

290

Every time I went to a place and couldn't find my son a pain rippled across my forehead.

It was all consuming.

I'm talking about the kind of pressure, if you could imagine, where a giant would have your head in his palms and squeeze tightly.

I hadn't eaten in two days. And the water that I drank came from stores that would take pity on me and give me a courtesy cup.

But I didn't want to eat.

I wanted my baby boy.

To this day I don't know what made me show up at her house. I'm not even sure why I thought she still lived there. But after exhausting all other resources, I returned to Nicole's apartment.

I would have gone to Penny's but she was on vacation, on a cruise, and no one could get a hold of her.

Talk about bad luck.

So I went to Nicole's and knocked on the door. Within seconds it opened and there she was with a smile on her face. She was wearing that white shirt, with that yellow smiley face again.

Suddenly, Greg walked behind her, kissed her on the cheek and walked down the steps.

"Yep...we together." She told me.

My jaw dropped. "Why?"

"Fuck you mean why? The dick. The man. Which part?"

"Nicole...I...I don't understand."

"Aw hush!" She waved her hand in front of my face. "We weren't together when they were together. But it happened right after Penny dumped him. I wanted him from the gate but he wouldn't leave Penny. So I had to get her to dump him." She nudged my shoulder. "Thanks, girl. You did that shit!"

I fucking hated that bitch.

But there were other things on my mind.

"Hey, uh...I know this is weird but has Peter been in contact with you?"

She smiled. "No." I didn't believe her.

"Okay...um, do you know how to get a hold of Penny? I really have to ask her something."

"I haven't spoken to that bitch since you left. Why you asking me?"

"Because...because." I could feel tears stream down my face. I felt so stupid for even having to come to my enemy with questions I

292

hadn't prepared. Afterall, what did I want from her?

Pity?

Help?

Love?

Things she never provided before.

"What do you want?" She said opening the door wider. "Because I'm busy."

"I want to..."

And that's when I saw my baby.

Playing in a playpen.

He looked happy.

He looked healthy.

And just that quickly the headache that consumed me vanished.

I moved to enter her apartment but she blocked me with a firm palm pressed into the center of my chest. Right between my breasts. Her fingernails scratched me lightly causing me to bleed a little.

I looked at her. Confused. Relieved. Angry. "What you doing with my baby?"

"You mean the baby you abandoned?" There was a look of satisfaction on her face again. And just like in the past, I could tell she was getting ready to destroy me verbally. "Is that the baby you talking about, bitch?"

"Nicole..." My entire body trembled like a vibrator. "I need my baby. Please hand him to me! We may have had our problems but this ain't right."

"He's actually in my custody now. Temporarily. Since we blood and all." She looked up. "Oh...and his father didn't want to take care of him either."

That hurt.

You couldn't even take care of our baby, Peter?

What man could be so cruel?

"Nicole, I'm back! Please open the door."

"Girl, you may be back but you still have to go through the processes and courts and shit. I'm not just gonna hand you a baby cause you asked for one."

Her happiness, which was a direct result of my pain, enraged me. My voice got deep. Calm and sure. "I'm coming inside to get my child."

"No you not either."

"I don't want to hurt you but I will, Nicole. I swear to God."

She started laughing.

Laughing in a way that she had before when we lived together. It was an awful laugh. Shrilly. Like fingernails crawling down a chalkboard.

It caused me to react.

Like I'd been possessed by an unseen force.

And so I tried to enter. But she pushed me back harder.

Finally, with the strength I still don't know how I came by to this day, I shoved her so hard that she went flying across the living room.

It was all slow motion.

And when it stopped, the side of her head crashed into the marble counter. The one from where she made me eat mayonnaise.

I may have hoped she was okay, but the blood from her wound that splattered onto my baby's face told me she wasn't.

Nicole died.

And to make a long story meaningful, I was charged with manslaughter. It was easy to put a case on me. Besides, I struck her before with a glass bottle. So it looked like I wanted her dead.

But being in jail was not rock bottom for me.

The bottom came when I tried to reach you.

About our son.

And you still didn't provide help.

Tye closed the book.

It was the first time she had addressed him directly.

Weirdly enough, reading the diary allowed him to understand her plight. To fight for her mentally all without knowing that he was the villain.

He reopened the cover.

Like I said, to make a long story meaningful, I was charged with manslaughter. I learned that you and Nicole came up with the plan together. You gave her fifteen thousand, and you took the rest. Of course it was easy. She told you about how gullible I had been with The Crying Game.

I was the perfect victim.

So you created another story to make me run. Complete with flour in trash bags in the closet. I must've been a joke.

Still laughing now?

Anyway, all I wanted was for you to get our son.

To get our child.

"Go get our baby," I begged.

296

You told me you wouldn't.

"I'll do whatever time I gotta do. But please don't let our son fall to the system. Please don't let him end up like you." I spoke.

Again, you said you couldn't be weighed down.

You said babies were weights of the world.

How could I forget?

You had already taken my money. That wasn't enough. You had to take my baby and soul.

There is no greater pain than being separated from your child. And you didn't care. You used me as a bank, which was used to pay your father's bail and fund drugs which landed you in prison.

I remember being excited when I heard the news. I felt I was finally getting some justice.

But you used some of the money to help your friends out on the street. Gave them money to keep them on their feet.

That made you a legend.

And then you beat your case.

Once again you were free.

I hated you for years. But my cousin Penny was right. I'm patient.

Very, very patient. Oh, and did I mention?

It took me some time. Ten years to be exact.

I waited.

Waited for you to build up the life you wanted. Let you get the girl. Let you get the business.

Before long it was Penny who found out where I was. She got my father's side of the family involved. Mainly my brother Posea. (No, that's not his real name)

And then I planned.

We planned.

Had my brother follow you from behind.

Waited for you to make a mistake.

They became allies.

Still are allies now.

You thought you happened to meet him by chance. Just as you needed the money to fund your restaurant.

But nothing is chance.

Luck is when preparation meets opportunity.

My opportunity.

You will now pay for what you did to me.

You will now pay for what you did to my son.

You will now pay for what you did to our lives.

298

Oh, and did I mention I'm free?

EPILOGUE
6 Months Later

Tye was sitting in his jail cell, literally staring at the wall. It was something he'd done more and more lately. He had been convicted of insurance fraud and sentenced to five years in prison.

Already he felt like he'd been in jail for years.

He had no idea when he flooded his restaurant that video cameras secretly recorded him. They were later given to the police, but only after the cashier's check was given to him, which he cashed and gave to Run.

He was a victim of his own kind of game.

A story made up in his honor.

Also known as a lie.

He was about to read one of his many novels when a member of the staff approached.

"Inmate, you have a visitor." The correctional officer opened the cell.

He turned his head in his direction.

He wasn't surprised.

He knew exactly who the visitor was.

Afterall, she was the only person on his list. His new favorite author. The one who successfully pulled him into the story of his own life.

His ex-girlfriend, Courtney Martin.

When he walked into the visiting hall, he sat across from Courtney. She was as beautiful as she was when they dated as teenagers and he couldn't help but smile. Light brown skin. Hazel eyes and pouty pink lips.

Ironically upon seeing his face, she grinned too.

"You know, I never thought you were ugly? Just needed to make you mad."

She didn't care. She no longer needed his approval. "So you put my name on your visitor's list," she placed her sandy brown hair behind her ear.

He looked down at the strawberry patch tattoo on her shoulder blade. Of course he remembered it now. But he had come in contact with so many women and tattoos over the years, that they all blended in with time. Not to mention the drugs and alcohol that became his diet.

"I had too. I wanted to see you." He clasped his hands in front of him.

She nodded. "Why?"

He eyed her tattoo again. "How did you know I would forget the tattoo?"

"Because you never really looked at me. Always through me."

He cleared his throat. "Why did you use the diary? Why couldn't you just tell me how you feel?"

"First off, I tried. Sent letters. Begged you to talk to me. You never had the time, remember? Because you didn't care."

"But you could've met me like–."

"I don't owe you shit. I used the diary because you treat people like characters. Always have. So I wanted to make you one in my world. How do you like it?"

He looked down. "I...I...at first I didn't understand how I could not see myself in that book but...but it's like life..."

"Life what, Tye?"

"I was on boat heavy back then and it fucked up my head. I haven't touched it since but–"

"Tye, why did you want to see me?"

"Because...because I wanted to tell you I'm sorry. For what I did to you. And what I did to our son."

His apology was real.

But it was too late.

"I deserve to be right where I am. And I accept that shit fully."

He saw her visibly change as he sat across from her. And whether she said it or not, he was grateful he could give her relief.

Or maybe it was revenge.

"Do you know where...where our son is?"

"I do."

"How is he?"

"Safe. With me." She exhaled. "But I won't tell you where. You don't deserve that honor."

He nodded. "So who is...Posea?"

She laughed. "He's my brother. Run. Don't bother asking the streets about him. Because if you turn the words around you'll notice it goes back to the fable. The Boy Who Cried Wolf."

She was right.

Aesop was the original author of the story. "Wow."

"So what now?"

"I'm running a podcast. Shared my story on it already. It's surprising how many people are going through the same shit. Maybe I'll help them too. An Ugly Girl's Diary, A Broke Nigga's Diary...the stories go on and on. People out here scamming and hurting others they think are weak."

"So you really see me as Peter? From the story."

She laughed. "Peter?" She leaned forward. "I used his name but of course you aren't Peter."

He frowned. "Then...then who am I?"

"I've always seen you as the wolf."

He looked down at his hands. Once again she checkmated his ass. He took her for gullible and had no idea how smart she was until this moment.

"So what happens now?"

"You mean are you safe?" She whispered. "Because of Logan? And the video we have of you arguing with him right before he was murdered? In your restaurant?" She sat back and grinned.

His jaw twitched. "Will this...will this come back on a nigga?"

"Keep your head down, Tye. Stay out the way. And maybe I'll stay out of your life." Slowly she leaned forward. "Because if you don't, if you go back to your old ways, don't be surprised if after five years you end up right back in here. There's no statute of limitations on murder. And there is no statute of limitations on what you did to my heart. Bye, *Peter.* For now." She got up and walked away.

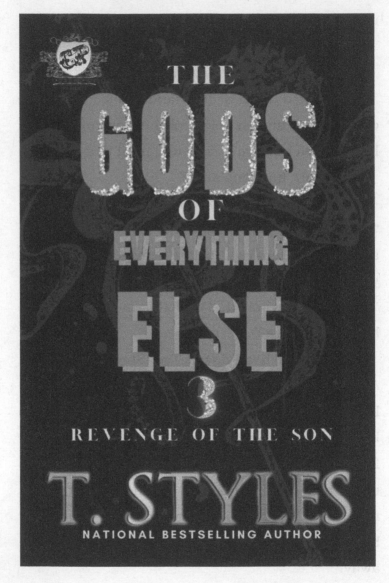

CARTEL PUBLICATIONS

PRESENTS

The Cartel Publications Order Form

www.thecartelpublications.com

Inmates **ONLY** receive novels for $12.00 per book **PLUS** shipping fee **PER BOOK.**

(Mail Order **MUST** come from inmate directly to receive discount)

Shyt List 1	_____	$15.00
Shyt List 2	_____	$15.00
Shyt List 3	_____	$15.00
Shyt List 4	_____	$15.00
Shyt List 5	_____	$15.00
Shyt List 6	_____	$15.00
Pitbulls In A Skirt	_____	$15.00
Pitbulls In A Skirt 2	_____	$15.00
Pitbulls In A Skirt 3	_____	$15.00
Pitbulls In A Skirt 4	_____	$15.00
Pitbulls In A Skirt 5	_____	$15.00
Victoria's Secret	_____	$15.00
Poison 1	_____	$15.00
Poison 2	_____	$15.00
Hell Razor Honeys	_____	$15.00
Hell Razor Honeys 2	_____	$15.00
A Hustler's Son	_____	$15.00
A Hustler's Son 2	_____	$15.00
Black and Ugly	_____	$15.00
Black and Ugly As Ever	_____	$15.00
Ms Wayne & The Queens of DC **(LGBTQ)**	_____	$15.00
Black And The Ugliest	_____	$15.00
Year Of The Crackmom	_____	$15.00
Deadheads	_____	$15.00
The Face That Launched A Thousand Bullets	_____	$15.00
The Unusual Suspects	_____	$15.00
Paid In Blood	_____	$15.00
Raunchy	_____	$15.00
Raunchy 2	_____	$15.00
Raunchy 3	_____	$15.00
Mad Maxxx (4th Book Raunchy Series)	_____	$15.00
Quita's Dayscare Center	_____	$15.00
Quita's Dayscare Center 2	_____	$15.00
Pretty Kings	_____	$15.00
Pretty Kings 2	_____	$15.00
Pretty Kings 3	_____	$15.00
Pretty Kings 4	_____	$15.00
Silence Of The Nine	_____	$15.00
Silence Of The Nine 2	_____	$15.00

Silence Of The Nine 3	_____	$15.00
Prison Throne	_____	$15.00
Drunk & Hot Girls	_____	$15.00
Hersband Material **(LGBTQ)** _	_____	$15.00
The End: How To Write A	_____	$15.00
Bestselling Novel In 30 Days (Non-Fiction Guide)		
Upscale Kittens	_____	$15.00
Wake & Bake Boys	_____	$15.00
Young & Dumb	_____	$15.00
Young & Dumb 2: Vyce's Getback	_____	$15.00
Tranny 911 **(LGBTQ)**	_____	$15.00
Tranny 911: Dixie's Rise **(LGBTQ)**	_____	$15.00
First Comes Love, Then Comes Murder	_____	$15.00
Luxury Tax	_____	$15.00
The Lying King	_____	$15.00
Crazy Kind Of Love	_____	$15.00
Goon	_____	$15.00
And They Call Me God	_____	$15.00
The Ungrateful Bastards	_____	$15.00
Lipstick Dom **(LGBTQ)**	_____	$15.00
A School of Dolls **(LGBTQ)**	_____	$15.00
Hoetic Justice	_____	$15.00
KALI: Raunchy Relived	_____	$15.00
(5th Book in Raunchy Series)		
Skeezers	_____	$15.00
Skeezers 2	_____	$15.00
You Kissed Me, Now I Own You	_____	$15.00
Nefarious	_____	$15.00
Redbone 3: The Rise of The Fold	_____	$15.00
The Fold (4th Redbone Book)	_____	$15.00
Clown Niggas	_____	$15.00
The One You Shouldn't Trust	_____	$15.00
The WHORE The Wind		
Blew My Way	_____	$15.00
She Brings The Worst Kind	_____	$15.00
The House That Crack Built	_____	$15.00
The House That Crack Built 2	_____	15.00
The House That Crack Built 3	_____	$15.00
The House That Crack Built 4	_____	$15.00
Level Up **(LGBTQ)**	_____	$15.00
Villains: It's Savage Season	_____	$15.00
Gay For My Bae	_____	$15.00
War	_____	$15.00
War 2: All Hell Breaks Loose	_____	$15.00
War 3: The Land Of The Lou's	_____	$15.00
War 4: Skull Island	_____	$15.00
War 5: Karma	_____	$15.00
War 6: Envy	_____	$15.00
War 7: Pink Cotton	_____	$15.00
Madjesty vs. Jayden (Novella)	_____	$8.99
You Left Me No Choice	_____	$15.00
Truce – A War Saga (War 8)	_____	$15.00
Ask The Streets For Mercy	_____	$15.00
Truce 2 (War 9)	_____	$15.00
An Ace and Walid Very, Very Bad Christmas (War 10)	_____	$15.00
Truce 3 – The Sins of The Fathers (War 11)	_____	$15.00
Truce 4: The Finale (War 12)	_____	$15.00
Treason	_____	$20.00
Treason 2	_____	$20.00
Hersband Material 2 **(LGBTQ)**	_____	$15.00
The Gods Of Everything Else (War 13)	_____	$15.00
The Gods Of Everything Else 2 (War 14)	_____	$15.00

Treason 3 $15.99
An Ugly Girl's Diary $15.99

(**Redbone 1 & 2** are **NOT** Cartel Publications novels and if <u>ordered</u> the cost is **FULL** price of $16.00 **each plus shipping**. <u>No Exceptions</u>.)

Please add **$7.00** for shipping and handling fees for up to **(2) BOOKS PER ORDER**. (INMATES INCLUDED) (See next page for details)

The Cartel Publications * P.O. BOX 486 OWINGS MILLS MD 21117

Name: _____

Address: _____

City/State: _____

Contact/Email: _____

Please allow 10-15 BUSINESS days Before shipping.

PLEASE NOTE DUE TO <u>COVID-19</u> SOME ORDERS MAY TAKE UP TO <u>3 WEEKS OR LONGER</u> BEFORE THEY SHIP

The Cartel Publications is <u>NOT</u> responsible for <u>Prison Orders</u> rejected!

<u>NO RETURNS and NO REFUNDS</u>
<u>NO PERSONAL CHECKS ACCEPTED</u>
<u>STAMPS NO LONGER ACCEPTED</u>